THE TALKING STONE

The Talking Stone

A MAGICALLY REAL
FANTSASY

BY
WILL BROOKE

Windwalker Books

The Talking Stone

Published by
Windwalker Books
Wheaton, Illinois

Design 2025 Windwalker Art

ISBN: 9781733910996 (eBook Edition)
ISBN: 9798218763947 (Hardcover Edition)
ISBN: 9798271132612 (Paperback Edition)

JUVENILE FICTION/Fantasy/Portals & Alternate Worlds

DOMINO DEO OMNIPOTENTI SOLI
DEDICATUM

Contents

Prologue

An old hermit sat at his workbench, focused on an object that, although small, worried him greatly.

He thought awhile, scratched behind one ear, and then after making some adjustments to the gadget with a slender tool, relaxed and said in a warm crackly voice, "Splendid, splendid, now let's see if you, my little guy, can focus enough dark wind to make my beautiful toy work again. I need to see what's going on out there. Today might be the day!" The hermit liked to talk to the things he tinkered with.

Strangely, he wouldn't or couldn't speak with anyone else, but he had a special affection for his inventions. So he talked to them constantly and cared for them as if they were his children. He carried the device into a cave lit by a shaft of light. It resembled a spotlight and shone on a brilliant console made of diamonds and glass. Standing in the center of the floor, it was the lens through which he saw between worlds.

Attaching the newly repaired part, he gently touched several places on the side of the device, and the console sprang to life in a whir of humming sounds and dazzling lights. Then he slid his fingers into an opening and began to move them gracefully, as if he were playing a musical instrument. An image appeared floating above the diamond surface, and the hermit's face brightened as a lad in his late teens came into view. He was walking down a sidewalk on a busy city street trying to press through a dense crowd.

The hermit made a few subtle hand motions, and the image changed to show the lad's face, then zoomed in on his eyes. They were curious, generous, and kind but skeptical.

"Yes," the hermit said. "Perfect, just in time, I think he's ready!"

The times when you see and are seen by another are like worlds spoken into existence; they are those unique connections that live on as unending treasures.
(From the Journals of Zambo the Mute)

[1]

Just An Ordinary Tuesday

RAAN GRABBED HIS KEYS and bounded down the stairs, excited because today was his day to explore. Skipping the bottom step, he hit the sidewalk at a trot, politely nodding to several pajama-clad neighbors squabbling over a parking spot. Pumped for adventure, he sped across the cobblestones heading south, leaving the autumn hues of Gramercy Park for another time.

He loved watching interesting people while exploring the neighborhoods of New York. But Raan avoided everyone and kept to himself, lost in his imagination, tracing sidewalks as if he were on the scent of buried treasure. A couple streets away, he saw some break dancers spinning on the sidewalk, and a few blocks farther, he dropped coins into the guitar case of a busker riffing on an old Gibson. But as he walked past the subway entrance at 14th and Union Square, he heard what he loved most: an underground drummer pounding infectious grooves in the tunnels. The beats echoed like thunder in hidden caverns.

He walked on, seeking mysterious and strangely angled streets and any unusual symbols carved into buildings. Today's exploration first took him east into Alphabet Town, but when he came upon two men settling an argument with a baseball bat, he decided to veer west toward Gansevoort Market and Greenwich Village.

The Village was one of Raan's favorite spots, filled with intriguing storefronts and narrow streets brimming with mysteriously carved doorways and signage. He passed by a restaurant boasting the best stromboli in New York, a tattoo parlor, and a florist adorned with so many wind chimes that it felt like a fantasy jungle overflowing with exotic fruit. Then, he noticed a shop he had never encountered before.

Passing the door of the Village Musical Instrument Emporium was like entering a parallel universe. The scent of incense and strange music greeted him, and he felt an unusual tingling excitement as he stepped across the threshold.

Every inch of the tiny shop was packed with the oddest musical instruments he had ever seen. Long, shapely sitars hung from the ceiling, antique guitars covered the walls, and bass fiddles and cellos were tucked carefully into corners. Hand-carved drums decorated with African symbols dotted the walls, and whistles, flutes, clarinets, and saxophones seemed to grow out of the shelves. The horn section dazzled his eyes with miles of shimmering brass and silver tubing. The entire store seemed alive and pulsing with creativity. It was almost magical.

Raan browsed this way and that, daydreaming about the sounds and music of faraway places, when two kind-looking men emerged from a back room. One was tall and thin with a bushy gray beard, and the other was short and heavyset, sporting a broad mustache and a smile as big as Texas. As Raan was examining a shelf filled with brightly painted Afghani cowbells, the men approached.

The tall man said, "Hello, greetings! Are you looking for anything in particular?"

"No, not really," said Raan, looking up from the cowbells, "just exploring, looking for a little adventure on an ordinary Tuesday."

"How interesting, you see we've been expecting someone fitting your description all day."

"We're so glad you've come at last," added the mustache man.

"Come at last, what do you mean?" said Raan as he sized up the pair. They didn't look dangerous, or creepy, just maybe a bit odd. But that describes many New Yorkers.

"We were told that a young man looking exactly like you would come here today to help us with a, shall we say, a rather delicate situation," said the short man with a smile.

"Who told you? What?" said Raan, who was getting ready to exit the shop and chalk the whole thing up to another weird New York encounter.

Then the tall man remarked, "There are secret worlds hidden in plain view, and the source of all adventure begins with someone who has the courage to take the first step."

"What?" said Raan, slightly aroused by the mention of secret worlds and courage. "What do you mean?"

"I think it's better if we show you," said the broad man. "Follow us."

Raan was wary about following the strangers but there was something about them that seemed, well, virtuous. He braced himself for the worst and followed, mostly because the strange magical tingling was growing in him, and that surprisingly, he had no fear, only an unexpected excitement.

The two men led him into a workshop in the back of the store. There were several benches lined with instruments in various states of repair, racks of tools, and shelves, but the odd thing was that the floor was entirely covered with sand—white sand nearly the color of salt.

The taller man said, "We appreciate you helping us with this. People with your kind of talent are very hard to come by."

"My kind of talent? What do you mean? Is this some kind of scam?" said Raan with his toughest New Yorker attitude.

"Absolutely not!" said the moustache man.

"Nothing but the noblest principles," said the other.

"What are you talking about? I need to be going," said Raan, looking toward the door.

"You'll figure it out along the way," said the first man calmly.

Before Raan could ask any more questions, the bearded man picked up a palm-sized djembe drum and tapped a complex rhythm with his fingers. At the same time, the moustache man played a series of notes on a brightly painted whistle. The floor trembled, and Raan felt a strange pulling on his body like a giant vacuum was drawing him into the sand. He and the two men sank knee-deep into the sandy floor that suddenly became soft and yielding. Raan regained his balance and tried to stand, brushing sand from his pants.

"We must apologize for how we are forced to travel," said the tall man, acting as if three men knee-deep in a sand dune in the back room of a Greenwich Village storefront were an everyday occurrence.

"This place is very difficult to reach, so we must use any means we can find," said the man with the mustache, shaking his leg as sand flowed off his shoe.

The first man continued, "It took us a long time to find you, and we know you are exactly the right person for the job."

"What job? This is insane! What's happening?" Raan asked as he clumsily tried to get his balance, bogged down in the shifting sand.

"You'll figure that out as you go," the shorter man interjected without missing a beat.

"But I—"

The tall man with the beard cut him off. "Everything in your life adds up to this one adventure."

"But I don't know what I'm doing or where I'm going," said Raan.

"Don't worry; you'll find help along the way."

Before he could respond, some unseen hole suddenly opened below, sand began to pour, and they were swept away. Raan was carried down the river of flowing white until he jolted suddenly and found himself sitting upright, buried in a haystack.

[2]

SOMEWHERE ODD, SOMEWHERE OLD

COLLECTING HIS WITS, Raan waited to see what would happen next. When all was still, he began to claw his way out, finally rolling onto solid ground, his clothes covered with hay.

He looked around him and saw row upon row of ordered haystacks running along the side of a long sloping field, bordered by forest on all sides. Up slope he could see mountains in the distance and down he saw the tops of interesting buildings with organically shaped rooflines poking over the trees. Brightly colored birds sang and swooped from the trees across the hay fields. The scent of fresh hay mingled with pine and hardwood made him think of a candle shop back home. There was no sound of traffic or machinery, so Raan thought this new world might be like his in the long past except that the sun was greenish-yellow surrounded by a deep blue aura. The lavender sky was eerie, looking a little like the horizon just after sunset only brighter.

As he brushed himself off, a tall, thin lad about his age walked up and said, “They sent me to look for you, and here you are sleeping in the hay? I’ll report that to the Grand Protector. Quick, no excuses; get yourself cleaned up. We’re late!”

Raan dusted his hair and clothes and realized they weren’t his clothes at all. This is getting stranger; he thought as he followed. The two lads hurried along a path leading from the fields into rich green woods. He noticed the buildings of a country village ahead. Suddenly, both lads noticed a bright shape on the ground before them. Rushing forward, the two grappled to seize the object. The tall boy lunged ahead, but Raan was a split second quicker, snatching it before the other. A tumbling, grabbing, wrestling match ensued; clutching arms and flailing legs knotted together as the lads rolled about on the trail. When it was over, Raan came out on top.

He held a strange stone at arm’s length for them to see. The stone was peculiar because it resembled a perfect teardrop; it was white and naturally shaped, not carved and crisscrossed with strange markings that seemed to be symbols of some kind.

"Give me that," said the tall kid. "Who do you think you are?" He grabbed for the stone, trying to wrestle it away from Raan, but the New Yorker's "don't mess with me" attitude arose, and he pushed his assailant away with a look so savage it could have fried an egg.

The tall lad stopped and studied Raan, bewildered. The sturdy New Yorker planted both feet firmly apart and prepared for the next attack.

"What's gotten into you?" the other lad said, relaxing and putting his hands in his pockets.

Raan stood motionless, saying nothing, fixing an intense gaze on the other, who cocked his head and said, "I'd like to throw that stone through the new stained-glass window in the House of Hearing's tower."

"That's a dumb idea," said Raan, not knowing what else to say. "I'll look at it later, maybe wear it around my neck. I think it's cool."

"Cool? Whatever! Come on, or they'll start without us.

[3] The Featherlight Disaster

RAAN PUSHED DOWN SOME less-than-polite thoughts and brushed more hay from his hair. *This is a bizarre way to start an adventure I didn't even ask for*, thought Raan as he followed the people flocking to the town's central market.

The market square was crowded with people, and the two young men pressed into the mass, working their way up to the front. Raan studied the faces around him, looking for the two men from the music emporium, wondering where those guys had disappeared to. On a broad platform stood an impressively dressed man with an enormous waist and a bright-red silken sash across his chest. He wore a greasy-looking black mustache with curled ends and a trim, pointed beard. He began speaking, booming over the crowd with the most authoritative voice Raan had ever heard.

"Ladies, gentlemen, boys, and girls, moms and dads, grandmas and grampas, visitors from near and far, friends, relatives, and of course, our esteemed clergy." As he said this final greeting, a flash of contempt crossed his face when he glanced at a gray-clad at the back of the crowd.

"Greetings, salutations, and welcome to all you citizens of our grand and illustrious land of Clallot!"

Raan wondered if this was going to be a long speech.

"Today marks the opening of our time-honored traditional featherlight regatta!" bellowed the man as cheers followed. "It was three decades ago today when my humble craft streaked to victory at our town's first race. I was just a boy, when under the most extreme difficulty, my robust featherlight sailboat navigated the treacherous river only to streak through—"

He would've gone on for who knows how long, but the honest-looking man in the back politely interrupted, "Could you, honorable Grand Protector, tell us the race's rules?" The man in the back wore a dark gray poncho, deep green trousers, with a thick leather belt with several pouches. He wore a silver emblem made of runes Raan didn't understand, clasped around his neck by a bright chain. He held a wide brimmed hat in one hand and a walking stick in the other.

"Yes, um, I was coming to that," said the Grand Protector.

As he explained the details of the competition and as people lined up to enter the race, the gray-clad man stood beside Raan, put his arm around his shoulders, and asked, "Are you planning on defending your title this year, son?"

Title? Son? I'm this guy's son, thought Raan. These people seem to know me. This adventure is becoming stranger. Raan worried about what they would do when they discovered he was an impostor and the real Raan appeared.

Raan unconsciously put his hand in his pocket and found the stone. It felt cool and smooth as he manipulated it between his thumb and fingers. Then, a strange thing happened: Raan's memory began to fill with the whole history of a life. It was like remembering a dream. Quickly, stories came into his mind that he'd never known, people he'd never met, events he'd never experienced, and places he'd never been. His New York life seemed distant and less real, and the old musical instrument shop and the two men became like a background story.

By way of his new memories, Raan learned that "Grand Protector" was what the townspeople of Clallot called their administrative leader. His name was Barredoch and he was mayor, governor, and chief problem solver, and he liked to be in everyone's business. The young man who' entered the town with him was Koal, Barredoch's son, and Raan's new dad was Seth.

All the featherlights in the race were in a tent near the town gates, and when Raan saw them, he couldn't believe his eyes. Their origami-like silk sails resembled an extravagant garden bursting with dazzling colors and design. One by one, contestants carried their featherlights to the river until only a single boat remained. Seth carefully handed the craft to him and said, "I'll meet you at the river. I have something I need to take care of. Good luck!"

Raan watched as his only friend in the strange world vanished behind a building and stood alone in this strange world holding an elaborate featherlight boat. Surveying his surroundings, he noted the direction of the last stragglers on their way to the river and wondered what he should do.

As he gazed at his ship, he noticed the intricate patterns and folds in the sails and how the brightly colored silk paper created lines and shapes that resembled complex art. Suddenly, more unexpected information flooded his mind: he realized that not only did the intricately folded sails catch the breeze, but they were also designed to harness an unseen flow of particles known as dark wind. The craft responded to the dark wind's force depending on the ultralight silk sail design. Each builder designed their unique sail pattern to catch the dark wind in a way that would propel their craft to victory.

The body of each featherlight was a thin but strong, hardened membrane that clung to the water's surface like a water bug clings to a pond. This way, the craft skimmed quickly over the water, using surface tension to keep it stable.

He could still see the last contestants and followed, hoping the two men from the music shop would be there so he could find out what was happening.

But before he'd traveled fifty steps, he met an elderly lady in a red babushka carrying a large canvas bag.

The bag lady's smile was beautiful—not like a toothpaste ad; more like your grandmother who just baked your favorite blueberry pie for your birthday. Her smile held a confident beauty that came from somewhere more enduring; not what she saw in the mirror but what she saw in the face looking at her. Raan knew she was smiling because he stopped to look at her. As bent as she was, her face beamed because some random young guy carrying a featherlight took time for her.

Raan noticed something about her that he would typically overlook in his busyness. Genuine kindness. They exchanged small talk while Raan fidgeted with the stone in his pocket; the race was about to begin, but he couldn't just dash away. As he unconsciously touched the stone, stories upon stories flooded Raan's mind, along with the woman's dreams, many joys, and pains. He wasn't ready for the wave of emotion.

He felt compassion, which was new to him. As he clutched the stone, more unknown knowledge about the woman flooded his mind, and empathy filled his heart. Once, she'd been beautiful and thriving, but now every one of her friends was gone, and she felt invisible. Yet she wasn't invisible at that moment, and it felt like heaven. For the first time in years, she felt noticed, and she thought, he sees me, and I see him. Events like featherlight races held no place in her mind, and the passing seasons meant nothing compared to something important: a conversation with someone new. Raan stopped fidgeting and settled in, giving this woman his full attention; this was more important than winning or losing.

"It's a lovely day," the woman said.

"Yes it is, perfect for a walk outdoors," said Raan, surprised with his polite words.

"Your name is Raan; I think, mine is Emma."

"Yes, I'm Raan. Pleased to meet you, Emma," said Raan, thinking the race was about to start, but feeling a strange warmth as he chatted with Emma.

"Yes, me too. I'm glad to make your acquaintance officially. Many of us know your name because you are always out and about fixing things with Seth. Where are you headed with that beautiful featherlight boat?"

"To today's race down by the river. It's about to start."

"Then you better get going! It was nice to finally meet you, officially. You must stop in for tea sometime soon; and bring your sister Casy," said the woman.

"I'll try, and look forward to talking with you again," said Raan as he began to back away.

When they'd finished their farewells, Raan raced to the river just in time to be the last to put his featherlight in the water. The wind was gusty, so at the last minute, he adjusted the sails and, in response to a random thought, tucked the white stone into the boat's body to give it greater stability—and they were off! His boat started at the back of the pack but slowly moved through the jumble of many craft. Some drifted off course, others succumbed to the gusts and floundered while Raan's featherlight knifed straight and steady over the water.

The excited crowd and contestants moved along the flat, grassy shoreline, watching the colorful sails and graceful ships sliding and bobbing in the wind. Out of the corner of his eye, Raan noticed Koal at the fringe of the crowd, talking to a few mean-looking men. Koal handed them something, and the characters disappeared across a bridge and into the trees opposite the lawn. From a distance, Raan caught a strange smirk on Koal's face before he looked away.

The river flowed along a sheer cliff opposite the riverbank. Several stony outcroppings stood along the cliff's edge like castle turrets watching over the scene below. Gleeful children and grownups raced along the lawn, jostling for the best view of their favorite craft. Women wearing colorful silk scarves mingled on the lawn, and men clad in their best clustered in small groups. A few enthusiastic youngsters who got too close to the shore were jostled into the flowing water, but the pushed became pullers, and all got a good soaking; bouncing out wet with feisty exuberance, feeling it all part of the fun!

Suddenly, a rumbling, crashing noise caused the crowd to look up. They were horrified to see great rocks from the cliff on the opposite bank tumbling toward the river and the featherlights. The landslide struck the water just as the regatta was underneath it, swamping many boats and knocking others into a chaotic jumble that spread out in all directions.

The crowd became a hubbub of confusion; teary-eyed children ran to their parents, and many stood gaping. Some called for the judges, others for the Grand Protector. Raan looked to the top of the cliff and thought he saw two men duck behind a boulder—the same men Koal had just been talking to before the race. He scanned the crowd for Koal and noticed he was rowing out to rescue the foundering boats.

A few of the sturdier craft survived; Raan's was among them, but there was no glory for any of the finishers in the wake of the tsunami.

Koal glowed with pride as he spoke with the crowd of admirers:

"Here, Alluu, take yours. I'm glad I was able to rescue it," said Koal handing a soaked featherlight to a grief-stricken boy. "And Mienimi, this one is yours, I think, better luck next time. Oh, Gossom, this yellow one is yours. There will always be next year." One by one, Koal distributed the waterlogged boats.

One of the kids came up to Koal crying and said, "I worked on this all year, and now it's ruined. Why did this happen?"

Koal avoided eye contact with the crying child and his parents but said, "Bad things happen to good people; you'll get over it Harii. I'm glad I was in the right place at the right time to save it. Now, whose is this green one?"

Koal continued comforting contestants, pairing soaked featherlights with their owners, and not so humbly receiving thanks for his quick action.

Koal beamed with excitement. "It was all in the timing. I just happened to be near the rowboat when the tragedy happened. Not thinking of my safety, I quickly leaped into action . . ."

[4] Secret Ingredient

RAAN AND SETH QUICKLY TIRED of Koal's bragging. They left the riverside and walked along a rutted clay street that led to a tree-lined lane. How weird, thought Raan. I've always wanted an adventure but never thought it would be like this. In the fading light, they arrived at a small building that seemed like a gathering place. In New York, it could be a church, but its angled walls and richly carved beams looked otherworldly. Behind it was a matching cottage that made him want to check if he was dreaming. He remembered that he was, after all, in another world.

He causally put his hand in his pocket and touched the stone, and new memories flooded into Raan. He learned that the building was called the

House of Hearing and that Seth was a Listener. A Listener was what Raan might think of as a priest or minister at home. A single stained-glass window in the House of Hearing's tower peered over them like an eye from heaven, and he thought this might be the eye Koal wanted to put out with the white stone.

As the men approached the cottage, Rann was surprised when they were met by three rambunctious animals resembling goats called gimmicks. They had the body and legs of a goat, but the head and tail of a cat. A pair with brown and gray spots nuzzled up to Seth, who treated them to a few morsels from his pocket. A black-and-white gimmick pressed its face against Raan's hip, but having no food, Raan just scratched the hairy animal between its ears, and the contented gimmick made a purring sound.

New memories continued to flood Raan's mind whenever he touched the stone, and his old life receded—the musical instrument shop and autumn bustle of New York dissolved into the cool night of the centuries-old fairy-tale town.

"Here we are," Seth said, opening the front door. "Casy, we're home!"

"Okay, just a minute. I'm just finishing up putting the secret ingredient into our stew," said a clear voice.

"Secret ingredient? Whose recipe is this?" asked the Seth.

"My own." Casy glanced toward them with a beaming smile that would make the Cheshire cat call its therapist.

Standing at a woodstove stirring something in a large pot was the prettiest girl—er, woman—he had ever seen. She wore a moonstone-colored smock, a bright red apron, and gray pants. Her braided hair was a blend of chestnut and wheat, and her eyes were like fiery sapphires. She had a crutch under one arm but moved about the kitchen as nimbly as if it were part of her.

"Your own recipe? I admire your creativity, dear, but you know I like to know what I'm eating," replied the hungry-looking man, putting his staff in a corner and hat on a peg.

"Okay," she said with a smile, "it's nothing."

"Nothing, of course. I'm sure it's no big deal, but I'd like to know," Seth inquired, more curious than ever.

"Nothing, really . . ."

"Now, you can have no secrets from your dad, even if you are my princess."

"Honest, Dad; it's nothing!" Casy looked awkwardly to Raan for help.

"I get it!" said Raan, finding his voice. "The secret ingredient is nothing. There is no secret ingredient."

"That's the secret." She winked, grabbing her crutch. Then, whisking over to her comically annoyed dad, she gave him a big hug.

"I know all your food allergies and wouldn't risk triggering anything." She stepped back to the stove and continued stirring and said with a playful grin, "Tonight's dinner is your favorite. Goose-dropping stew."

He launched a cushion at her head but intentionally missed, and the two busied themselves setting the table for dinner.

"Can I help?" asked Raan, feeling like an extra gear in a finely oiled machine.

"Of course, silly. You can do the dishes as usual."

Dishes, ugh. I guess I can learn anything, he grumbled to himself, beginning to realize that adventures were more than slaying dragons.

Raan saw that the cottage was cozy and clean, and the smell of the wood fire and fresh bread filled him with a desire to sink into the nearest chair and crack open a book. The memories of two worlds mingled in his mind, like the vague impressions of a movie he hadn't seen in years.

Bright light danced all over a large open room from plenty of oil lamps, and at one end was an expansive stone fireplace and mantel. Opposite was the kitchen. Between was a long, sturdy table with candles that looked like honeycombs and earthenware plates and bowls of all sorts. Near the hearth were comfortable chairs, and everywhere were shelves of books, cupboards, sideboards, and racks. Beds were in the corners and tucked into lofts in the rafters. The whole place seemed snug, homey, and more comforting than anyplace Raan had ever been.

That night, the three sat pensively around the blaze of the wood fire.

"What a horrible day!" said Casy after Seth explained the tragedy at the regatta. "Did you see the faces of those heartbroken people? All their hard work was swamped. How unlucky those rocks crashed into the river."

"Unlucky?" said Seth with a queer look, "Unlucky, yes, but those stones have stood on those cliffs for a thousand years. It's an interesting coincidence, wouldn't you say?" He looked into Casy's bright eyes and then at Raan, who stared into the fire. "Did you notice anything strange, Raan?"

Raan remembered the mischievous look on Koal's face just before the incident, the men talking to Koal, and the glimpse of someone atop the cliff.

"I can't be sure of anything, but I thought I saw someone on top of the ridge after the landslide," said

Raan, trying not to say who he thought was behind the catastrophe.

Casy interrupted, "At least Koal recovered the swamped boats."

"Indeed, today's hero was there in the nick of time," said Seth dubiously.

"Yes, he had a rowboat ready to go so he could reach them before they sank," said Casy, as she stuck her tongue in her cheek, thinking about all the unlikely coincidences.

"Yes, it's very convenient Koal was in the right place at the right time. The boats will all sail again, but the beautiful clifftop is now only a memory," said Seth, stroking his chin.

That night, Raan lay staring at the ceiling. A stray 'spiderweb dangled like a lonely trapeze amid ghostly shadows of rafters silhouetted in the fading firelight. His thoughts flitted among many things, like the two men Raan saw at the top of the cliff after the disaster, and his secret, but they kept returning to the questions, What happened to the men from the music shop, and how he would get back home?

Raan drew the white stone from his pocket. He looked at it awhile and thought about his suspicions that Koal had staged the whole thing just to play the rescuer. He longed for the truth and was bugged thinking that Koal could get away with a stunt like that without anyone noticing. The nerve, he thought. But why?

With his mind swirling, he sank into his mattress and like butter on fresh baked bread, melted into the pillow. Why did he always think about food when he was stressed? He also felt uncomfortable not being in control and thought, Adventures have their drawbacks.

Brilliant sunlight drenched Casy's face as she urgently poked Raan's shoulder.

"Wake up, silly. It's almost time for the House of Hearing!"

"Okay, I'm awake," he half-lied, stumbling out of bed, scratching his head, and stretching as a big yawn overcame him.

He quickly got ready and fell in line with Seth and Casy, throwing a piece of last night's bread into his mouth. The House of Hearing was almost filled with good-natured faces. A few smiled a forced polite smile to Raan and nodded; others smiled honestly, the kind of smile you smile when you know a secret.

The morning in the House of Hearing was hard for Raan to describe. Enchanting music played constantly—it was sometimes energetic, other times deeply haunting. People sang or respectfully listened to what he learned was the Voice. Raan was swept away in the experience. The Listener's talk was short and relevant, but Raan remembered few details, mostly how it made him feel—inspired with purpose and meaning, better than he'd felt in years. But he noted that it seemed weird to feel this way on Sunday morning, if it was Sunday in this world. At home church had always been an intellectual thing for him, but this was different, and unnerving, because it was something he couldn't control.

[5]
An Unusual Family

RAAN TOOK HIS NEW LIFE IN stride. He fell into a rhythm, working alongside Seth with knowledge that miraculously flowed into his memory. What else could he do? He had no way of contacting the men from the music emporium or figuring out a way back on his own.

At first he found it helpful to think everything around him wasn't real, so for a little while, he kept it all at arm's length, but after a stubbed toe and an aching back from a hard day's work, his ideas of reality quickly changed. The honest physical pain of a working person was the most real thing he'd ever experienced.

Seth was the perfect example of a rebel-saint nice guy, a theology professor, and a Jedi master. Think Han Solo and Yoda combined with Mr. Rogers—with a tool pouch instead of a lightsaber. Sundays, he preached the Way of the Voice, which is to treat others as you'd like to be treated.

Seth put the Way into practice during the week as the village handyman, fixing every broken gadget from farm or workshop and mending every problem known to man or machine. And any time of the week, sometimes day and night, you'd find him comforting the sick and assisting those who needed help. Yet he was quick to acknowledge his shortcomings and valued a good joke and laugh.

You'd find Seth reading in his spare time, and he loved his time studying law when he was younger. After talking with Seth, a person responded more to how he listened than what he said, though when asked for advice, he was considerate and wise. Almost everyone liked him—well, everyone but the Grand Protector and the Qerds. He was intentionally left out of town meetings and branded a radical because he didn't give unquestioning lip service to Barredoch.

Raan quickly fell in step with Seth's handyman business and became a regular sight around town, carrying tools or materials and taking on simpler jobs while assisting with major projects. Raan wasn't sure how to unpack Seth's version of faith. Before his journey, he thought religion was mostly smoke and mirrors with ample guilt thrown in to make a person feel justifiably miserable most of the time. This was different. He wondered if he didn't like this new religion less because it made him feel smaller and see everyone else as more important than himself.

Raan learned that Casy was generous with her patience and quick to join in the liveliest conversation. Around the table, it was often Casy's wise words that settled a controversy. Her crutch blended into her every movement, and she carried the attitude that it didn't matter. Although she didn't intend it, her virtue and courage inspired the townspeople to adopt attitudes of love and goodness they wouldn't have on their own.

Once a week Casy would drive her cart to the town square and invite people to bring excess food, clothing, and useful goods to share with those who were in need. When she'd collected enough, she would drive to 'the homes of people who were forced into poverty by circumstances beyond their control—especially those who could not work or people coping with illness, abuse, or disability—and share the generosity of the townspeople. Some folks were regular givers, others gave when they had extra, but everything was done quietly with respect. Casy told Raan that she had little patience for those who were living in poverty because they wouldn't work for various reasons. "We all make our choices," were her words.

Raan respected that she was fearless and unafraid to stand up to bullies like Koal or his thugs—like how she responded when Koal stole a blossom from every garden in town and gifted her with a huge mixed bouquet before asking her to the summer dance. She kindly accepted the flowers but declined his invitation. "The dance sounds wonderful, but I might accidentally trip one of the girls with my crutch or make someone uncomfortable. Thanks for the flowers; they're so bright and cheerful. But Koal, will you do me a favor? I've baked a big batch of cookies for the dance. Will you take the tray with you when you go?"

Koal looked at his shoes, Raan thought he might be wondering if he was too important to be a cookie delivery man.

"Women!" Raan heard Koal mutter. as he walked away with a fresh-baked tray of sugar-frosted kolu-chka on his shoulder.

[6]
A Plot Discovered

SETH AND CASY'S HOME was an A-frame structure with many gables carved with geometric patterns that resembled Arabic or Celtic art. Its doors and windows were triangular shapes that made the house a perfect fit for the mountain forest terrain. It looked very sturdy. Indoors, there were carpets and fabric art everywhere that were exquisitely patterned with vibrant color. The home was adorned with richly worked wood and stone. Behind the house was a two-story barn that housed the animals. The upper story contained supplies, and below, carved into the side of the hill, were the stables.

Washing dishes wasn't the only chore Raan had to learn in the new world. Barnyard work was an eye opener. Seth and Casy kept two dairy cow-like animals called mau. They had colorful feathery manes and tails. Casy named the mau Squirts and Cheese. Underfoot there was a pair of hupipops: creatures that looked like oversized Barnevelder chickens with fur instead of feathers. Casy called them Drumsticks and Wings. There were also two small eggaloos that resembled laying hens, except they had a tiny trunk in the place of a beak; the eggaloos had the fitting names of Omelets and Scrambles. There was also a plump grumpy blube they called Chopps, and the three cantankerous spotted gimmicks named Moe, Larry, and Curly, who Raan had met the night before. Casy trained all the animals to come to the names she'd given them.

Raan's first day of barnyard work was a disaster.

"It's your turn to milk the mau. Here's the bucket," said Casy handing a pail to Raan and busying herself with other morning tasks.

Raan stood frozen, looking at the enormous animal and its swollen udder.

Casy chimed in, "They're ready to burst"; you must have forgotten how to do your favorite job. Remember, whoever does the milking has first dibs on the cream"

He walked over to the two mau, who aimlessly chomped in their feed box. He reached for the stone and realized he'd left it in the house. Luckly, he remembered a video he once saw describing how to milk a cow, so with the vague notion of the process, he grabbed a stool and set to work.

"Okay, what's next," said Raan proud of the full pail of fresh milk. No one noticed one of his pant legs was soaked, and there was a wet spot in the turf. The milk's sweet aroma lured him to take a sip, but Raan resisted.

"As if you don't know? You taught me how. To forage the gran, silly. Are you Okay? The blube seems calm this morning. Lucky you!"

"I'm all right," said Raan, "just a little drowsy."

A blube was a cross between a walrus and a sow. From one of his memory downloads with the stone, Raan knew that the animal had a pouch like a kangaroo from which people would harvest an oatmeal-like substance called gran that had the scent of cinnamon when dried and burned. Casy made the gran into cones and sold the precious incense at market.

However, blubes could be temperamental, and even the slightest disturbance could be dangerous. The trick was to tenderly rub its chest and get the animal to lie on its back. Then while continuing to stroke the blube's chest, reach an arm into the pouch and extract a handful of gran.

Raan talked softly to the animal, "Okay Chopps, steady, old gal, we can do this." And as he stroked Chopp's chest, the beast rolled over on her back. "Well done good gal, now for the fun part." But as hard as he tried, Raan couldn't make himself put his hand inside the blube's pouch. Don't embarrass yourself, just do it! he thought, but his hand wouldn't move. He kept stroking Chopp's chest, and the animal remained relaxed.

"I don't know what's gotten into you today Raan, you've done this a thousand times," said Casy kindly as she knelt next to them. "I'll do it, you keep Chopps calm." Soon they had a pot full of gran and Casy said, "I'll go get cleaned up and put this on the stove to dry. Are you sure you're okay?"

"Just a little tired, I'll be okay. Thanks for helping!" said Raan, thinking that adventures aren't all slaying dragons, and wondering if there were Pop-Tarts in this world.

***

Late one evening, a boy came to their door, panting and very excited.

"We've got a terrible problem down at the fountain. There's no water. We pump and pump- and nothing comes. Half the town is gathered, and people are starting to fight, accusing each other of breaking the pump. Can you do anything?"

"I'll go," said Raan, looking at Seth, who was wrapped in a blanket. The two men talked a few minutes; Raan grabbed a bag of tools and some parts and headed out with the lad.

After an hour, he had the pump going, and the townspeople jostled in line for water. Some grumbled it had taken too long. Others complained that they don't make pumps like they used to.

Raan walked home the long way, hoping to enjoy the evening air and a little time alone. His trek took him past City Hall, where he noticed an ornate ebony carriage with twin horses and coachman on the side of the building near the Grand Protector's private entrance. Two elegantly dressed men stood at the doorstep. Something about two well-dressed men in that part of town at that time of night seemed unusual, so Raan moved in for a closer view and stood in the shadows under the feed store awning as the men cautiously looked around the street before entering.

The night was quiet, and Raan drew near a window unnoticed and watched. He felt uncomfortable and worried about getting discovered spying, but he couldn't help himself. Was the stone leading him?

A single candle pierced the room's darkness, creating a dome of light on the tabletop; everywhere else was masked in shadow.

"Let me get some lamps," said Barredoch standing nervously, unconsciously cracking his knuckles.

"We've enough light," said a smooth voice that made Raan shiver.

"To whom do I have the honor of—" The Grand Protector was cut short by another man who carried a polished black walking stick with a head that glimmered gold in the candlelight.

"We'd like our little meeting to go unnoticed. I'm sure you understand," said the man, placing a small stack of gold coins on the table. Raan noticed an intricate ring on his hand, bearing an ornate crest. Maybe one of the silk merchant families, he thought.

"Of course, but it's late," said Barredoch, eying the coins. "What is this all about?"

"Only a deal," said the man with the stick.

"What deal?" said the Grand Protector, trying to keep his dignity while taken aback that someone would be so bold to approach him.

"What would you say if all the silk of your town's farmers came to one buyer for one price, under your control? It would then be sold to our customers far away. Of course, you would get a percentage of the whole business. Does that sound interesting?"

"But that would disrupt the free trade of all the family businesses in our region. They've been farming and weaving silk independently for generations. They'd never agree," said Barredoch.

"I'm sure someone as resourceful as yourself could find a way to persuade them. We only need standardization and on-time delivery."

"But our silk is the finest hand-crafted cloth in the country, and our carpets have no equal—many of our customers are royalty!" said the Grand Protector.

"Maybe so, maybe so," said the smooth-talking man with the stick, "but what do you, their industrious and dynamic leader, get out of it? There are taxes, but they go to the king. What if you received something for yourself from every sale? In our markets, people can't tell good silk from bad and we're only concerned with volume."

"And profits," said the other. "Did we mention you get a percentage?"

There was a pause, and the candle flickered.

"But how can this be done?" the Grand Protector quickly glanced at the coins and then into a dark space between the men.

The first man leaned in. "There are many ways."

The second said, "Build big barns and factories; put the children to work in one place for long hours."

"But the people will never agree," said the Barredoch, puffing up his chest and clearing his throat.

"Convince them it's progress."

"Or fashionable."

"Invent a crisis. A common cause."

"Inflame a sense of pride or public duty."

"Create a competition."

"Offer key influencers part of the profits."

"And make them forget how wonderful life is now and create an urgent need in them to do what you want."

"There are many ways," said the man with the ring.

Barredoch pulled his beard thoughtfully and looked toward the black outline of the window. Raan ducked back. The Grand Protector rose to his full height and stretched his neck up to seem taller. "Your idea is intriguing; I'll consider it, but for the moment, I have pressing business."

"Consider well, but not too long. There are other towns," said the ring-wearer, retrieving the coins.

Raan slipped into the shadows as the men drove off. He walked home, reeling from what he had just seen and heard. He reached into his pocket and felt the smooth surface of the stone. He remembered there was something behind all that was in play, and that gave him a little comfort.

The following day, Seth's eyes burned with indignation when Raan told the story. Casy was outraged. "Of all the foul ideas. Working children and robbing families of their dignity to run their own farms. Turning our beautiful town into an industrial zone!"

"What did you say?" said Raan, trying to catch Casy's eye. Did she say industrial zone? Rann thought.

"It's tragic!" continued the hot-headed woman, avoiding Raan's question and his gaze. "We have to do something!"

"Yes, this is serious," said Seth with a flame in his eyes. "I'll make some inquiries tomorrow and see what I can find out; we'll talk about it later."

Raan began to wonder about his mission. Was this it?

Faith believes the Divine mysteries are intentional ambiguities placed in life to draw us to higher thought and noble deeds. It's much the same with personal suffering; our troubles help us feel compassion for others.
(From the Journals of Zambo the Mute)

[7] THE FIRE AND THE WIND

THE BIBGIT COLONY WAS on the outskirts of town near the river. Raan would pass through it traveling to outlying farms and was on polite terms with all the Bibgits, well at least on nodding terms, but he didn't understand their ways. He didn't fear them in the least; they only seemed distant and unconcerned with anything but their own affairs. They never stopped to talk and usually slipped away when townspeople came near.

Raan knew why most townsfolk didn't like them. They were different. For one thing, they laughed a lot, usually not at anyone or anything. They just laughed out of sheer joy. This made the townsfolk uncomfortable, feeling they weren't in on the joke.

Another thing was that they spoke directly—not in a mean sort of way but clearly with honest emotion, unafraid to say something embarrassing. They might say, without any meanness, Why are you fat? or Your dog is ugly, or My brother has smelly gas today. This struck fear into the hearts of an ordinary person in town, knowing a Bibgit could blurt out anything at any time.

They weren't welcome at parties or gatherings, as someone's social status was sure to crumble if any Bibgits were present, except as domestic help.

Bibgits tended to be short, with broad faces and big eyes. They were very clever and nimble with their fingers, quick to understand puzzles, and good at solving problems and fixing things. Raan rarely had handyman jobs among Bibgits.

The night of the fire was cloudless and windless. Perhaps that's why the blaze spread the way it did. Raan was on his way home after repairing a door latch in a cottage upriver. As he walked by the colony, he heard a tremendous roar. Raan sprinted to the scene to find a crowd of Bibgits frozen in shock as tongues of flame completely engulfed a barn and sprang from the upper windows and roof of a nearby house. As clever as they were, Bibgits had a profound fear of fire and were seized with terror. Suddenly, Raan heard a cry from inside the flaming house.

"Someone's inside!" he called out, but no one moved.

Raan put his hand in his pocket and unconsciously grasped the stone. Whether it was foolishness or a flood of unexpected courage, his instincts took over, and the lad dashed to a nearby water barrel, soaked his clothes, and ran to the burning house.

He kicked the door in and was instantly blinded by smoke; he fell to the floor, where he could see and breathe better. The roar was deafening, but he called out and heard a faint response from across the room. Smoke stung his eyes. It seemed like miles, but he crawled over the hot floor until he found two small children and their mother curled in a corner, disoriented by heat and smoke. Raan reached out and touched each of them, said it would be okay, touched the stone, and prayed for help! He heard a calm voice in his mind saying crawl, now! Across the room, Raan saw the light of the doorway penetrating the smoke.

"Hold on to my belt!" he said to the first child. "Hold your brother's belt!" he told the other. "Mom, you stay close behind!"

Raan led the family across the floor through a tunnel of flame. He waited at the door while the family passed in front of him, but just as they passed through, the wall behind them collapsed, and a flaming lintel crushed Raan to the floor. Twisting free of the flaming beam, he dashed into the open with his clothes on fire. Onlookers gaped, but some threw buckets of water onto him as he rolled in the dirt. A searing pain on his back made him leap up, sprint to the river, and plunge himself in.

Meanwhile, the fire continued to rage, and flames began to lick nearby houses, threatening to spread to the rest of the colony's wooden buildings. Raan looked up from the cold river water and unconsciously babbled a desperate plea, "God, if you are real, please help these people."

No one noticed it at first, but soon, people could see that the wind began to blow. Wherever the flames tried to reach a nearby house, the wind blew in the opposite direction and pushed them back. If they reached north, the north wind would push them back; if they stretched south, an opposing wind would protect the neighbor's house.

Night fell as the fire burned itself out and ghostly columns of blue smoke rose from the charred remains of the burned home. People huddled in small groups, quietly talking. The soot-covered faces of two kids and their mom exploded with joy to see their father pressing through the crowd. His grateful tears washed their exhausted faces.

Suddenly, the clamor of a harsh bell and horses captured everyone's attention as a wagon of townspeople raced to the scene led by none other than the Grand Protector and his son. Leaping from the stopping wagon, Koal cried, "The cavalry has arrived." But he was underwhelmed with his reception. He continued to boast, "We have blankets and food for all who have suffered." He looked over the victims, who already had plenty of food and warm blankets. During the long pause of awkward silence, Raan hobbled up. His hair was a tangled mess; his clothes were soiled, torn, and burned; and he limped up looking as if wild elephants had just trampled him.

"And who do we have here? A sorry sight!" said Koal, oblivious to what had happened and heedless of the praises Raan received from the Bibgit crowd. "Crawling in the dirt and swimming when there's work to be done."

Raan took a deep breath, sighed, and after a warm nod to the mom and her family, smiled at Koal and said, "I've been a little busy." With that, he picked up his tool bag and headed home.

The following day as Raan walked home from the doctor, he saw a notice on the town bulletin board describing the events of last night's fire and the heroic efforts of the fire brigade, who provided blankets, food, and much-needed moral support to those affected by the terrible catastrophe. An appeal was made for donations made in the care of the Grand Protector's office. The rescue wasn't mentioned.

[8] Blackmailed

THE CANDLES ON THE Grand Protector's desk flickered and crackled faintly, sending ghost-like shadows dancing on the ceiling. Its fiery glow sparkled in Barredoch's eyes as he sat like a cornered animal, waiting.

A small group of gnarled men sat on heavy wooden chairs opposite him. Their intent and hard faces were set apart by the birthmark that ran from the top of their nose over their forehead, revealing they were Qerds. Most townspeople hated the Qerds because many of them were henchmen for Barredoch. Their resentment was intensified because many Qerds considered themselves aloof and often condescended to; the townspeople tried to ignore them.

One of the men was chewing something he never swallowed; another unconsciously tapped on the desktop as if drumming to some inner music; a third clenched a wide-bowled pipe between his teeth and searched for a matchstick in his pocket. Their eyes were like lances. Barredoch squirmed slightly, adjusted his collar, and unconsciously ran his hand through his hair. Clearing his throat, he spoke. "Gentlemen, gentlemen, everything is going according to plan, just as we agreed."

Chairs creaked, and the men's feet shuffled. A tall, dark-haired man named Blemósh drew on his pipe and blew a thick cloud of smoke toward the Grand Protector, who held back a cough.

"So you say," said the smoker, "but words flow too easy from your mouth. We need something real." Smoke streamed from his nostrils.

"What can be more real than what I've already given you?" said the Grand Protector.

"The price has gone up," said the chewing man, leaning forward.

"This is outrageous. I can hardly afford—" Barredoch was cut short when the third man spat. "We wonder what the people would think if news about your little secret came out."

"The people would never believe rumors about their beloved leader," said Barredoch, nervously stroking his chin beard, knowing he was in a tight spot.

"Of course not, and if accidents stopped happening to those who disagree with you, perhaps nothing would change, perhaps," said the table-tapper, taking a deep breath so that his massive chest rose to meet his prickly chin.

"And, of course, people will gladly pay all their taxes without, shall we say, incentives," said the smoker, knocking ashes onto the floor. "We know you want to keep your promises," he added, "so we can keep ours."

"Alright, alright, let's talk about it," stalled the Grand Protector, buying time to think. "I've been considering adjusting your bonuses for all your quality work," he said, straightening the papers on his desk. "Just keep your side of the bargain. I have something in the works that will secure everything—something that will turn out profitably for us all." A curious smile curled under the Grand Protector's prim mustache.

"I just learned something new that may work to our benefit," said Barredoch thinking about his conversation with the silk barons. "It's too soon to talk about the plan but it will be very profitable.

To start, we just need to begin to find a way to unite the people against a common enemy." Barredoch swirled his moustache and thought. Quickly he said, "Maybe it could leak to some of the more talkative towns folk that Seth and Raan have a plan to steal the prince's treasure. Can I count on you fine gentlemen to spread news about this evil plot?"

Barredoch relaxed after the men left. *Why did it need to be so complicated*?. He wished he could only get the guilt off his chest, but he thought confession and forgiveness were just a bunch of religious nonsense. Yet he almost wished it were true.

He closed his office and walked home in the darkness wondering how Koal was doing on his mission. He was proud of his son, but he never let it show. Despite Koal's shortcomings, the lad was resourceful and willing to do what was necessary. *At least he's following in my footsteps,* thought Barredoch. Thinking about Koal made him revisit his past and less complicated times. He thought back to his carefree days and wondered where he'd lost them. Then he remembered a poem he'd memorized as a child:

You came to me begging bread,

I've given you a banquet.

You've gathered crumbs under
my table,

I've placed you in a seat of honor.

As the sun rises,

and the stars shine,

the waters will never cover you,

because I will never leave.

He never really understood that poem, but it always made him feel good. Pushing back his memories of simpler times, he slumped into bed fell into dreams about the Prince's hidden treasure.

[9]
Freeing Mr. Crickles

Casy kept a pet cricket named Mr. Crickles. She discovered the creature near the stack of firewood when she heard it chirping, saying, at least to Casy, "I'm lost and wounded. Can someone help me?" When she found the insect, it was in dire straits with a foreleg missing and one of its hind jumping legs badly damaged.

With Seth's help, Casy made Crickles a house out of reeds and twigs and did her best to make it as much like home she could. She was annoyed when Raan said it looked like a fancy cage, and thought, What do guys know? In a corner, they put cricket food—tiny bits of potato, grain, and fruit—in another corner was a thin leaf, curled at the edges, forming a cricket-sized basin containing a few drops of water. The house was furnished with pebbles, small stones, and a few sticks and greenery for cover, making it as cozy as any cricket could want as far as she knew.

Over the next few weeks, Crickles chirped, crawled, ate, and seemed to regain strength. Casy talked to her pet throughout the day and enjoyed its company until something unexpected happened.

While preparing dinner, Casy heard a strange popping sound coming from Mr. Crickles's house. It happened several times, and she discovered Mr. Crickles was jumping! Its leg was healed, and the cricket smashed into the ceiling of his house each time it tried to hop. Casy was overjoyed but perplexed. The jumping was an answered prayer, but now the chirps meant, "I'm trapped; set me free." Casy's heart dropped, torn between love for her pet and the thought that she was keeping it prisoner.

She made up her mind to give Mr. Crickles a choice: to stay with her or to return to the wild.

The next sunny day, Casy took the cricket house, set it on a log at the edge of the woods, and opened the door. Carefully, she took out Mr. Crickles, put him on the log, and waited in the shadow of a tree. At first the cricket did nothing; she imagined Crickles engaged in an inner debate not knowing what to choose.

Casy noticed a bluejay land on a tree branch nearby, its head twitching from side to side, looking for its next meal. A second later, she heard the deep-throated croak of a frog she noticed, carefully moving in the shadows under the log, and her eye caught the cunning motion of a snake gliding through the grass in the direction of the lonely cricket.

Suddenly, the bluebird swooped down from its perch, thinking a juicy cricket would make an excellent meal, and Casy yelled, "Look out." That was enough to frighten the bird, but Mr. Crickles remained motionless, perhaps frozen with fear. The snake was beginning to climb onto the log, and the frog hopped within striking distance. Casy called out, "Go back into your house, and you'll be safe!" but Crickles didn't respond. As the bluebird launched into the air for another strike, the frog flicked its sticky tongue toward the cricket in a near miss, and the snake slid its way past the little house and opened its mouth to strike. Suddenly, Casy launched her crutch at the log with all her might. The cricket was startled by the crash and jumped just out of reach of the diving bird. The frightened snake disappeared, and the frog hopped into the brush. Mr. Crickles was nowhere to be seen.

That night, Casy told her story to the guys.

Raan said, "If only you could speak cricket, you could have warned Mr. Crickles about the dangers."

"I thought he could feel my love for him and understand my heart," said Casy, holding back her tears. "I guess I'm just being silly, hoping for something like that. How can anyone know the heart of another?"

"Love is a complicated language for anyone to understand, especially between a cricket and a person," said Seth.

"Yeah, if you were a cricket, he'd understand. At least he got away!" said Raan.

"True, but I'm not a cricket, and even if I were, I'd be dodging frogs, snakes, and birds just like he was. It wouldn't be the same. Still, it's all nature. The cycle of life and all that."

"Yes, if you became like him, you could teach him many things," said Seth.

"And I'm sure he could teach me some cricket tricks too," said Casy, imagining what it'd be like to jump thirty times her body length.

"But there's still the risk, and as a cricket, you could no longer do people stuff," said Raan.

"Yes, but somebody had to help him." Casy silently reasoned, I wish I could tell them what is really bothering me, but they wouldn't believe me. They seem safe and strong, but they wouldn't understand.

Seth said, winking, "It's funny, Casy; your idea reminds me of another story I heard from the old hermit across the mountain."

The two young people looked at each other. Seth's stories were legendary. Raan put his hands in his pockets, and Casy adjusted her hair and waited entranced. Seth opened his mouth to speak, just as an enormous crack of thunder startled them back into the present.

Seth ran to the front door and saw dark clouds rolling in over the treetops, now swaying in a ferocious wind. They saw a greenish tint in the ebbing twilight and smelled a tinge of ozone in the air.

"It's a big storm; tie everything down you can!" called Seth, reaching to close the shutters as fast as he could.

"I've got the animals!" yelled Raan above the wind, seeing loose branches and debris flying horizontally across the lawn. He gathered the animals into the barn and battened the doors.

"I'll get fresh candles and buckets for the leaks," cried Casy, whose voice could hardly be heard above the din.

Before long, they all sat snug around the fireplace, and the angry voice of the storm roared.

[10]
An Unexpected Guest

THE HOWLING WIND and rolling thunder rattled the stone walls of the cottage. They expected the roof to fly off any minute. No one slept. In a catechesis of pounding rain and crashing tree limbs, Raan did just about the only thing he could; he tried to pray.

"If somebody is there, please help us!"

A single lamp swinging from a trembling rafter sent shadows darting throughout the room. Lightning flashes pierced gaps in the shuttered windows. Between thunderclaps, they could hear Seth's steady voice defying chaos with quiet words of timeless verse.

Raan was out at first light, inspecting for damage and collecting downed branches around the property. When retrieving a large limb from behind the bell tower, he noticed that the small wooden door to the coal chute was open a crack. As he drew near to shut it, he heard someone passionately arguing inside. Sneaking closer, Raan listened to a heated conversation within—but he could only hear one voice.

Seth had already left for town, and Casy was in the house, so who was in the cellar under the House of Hearing? Raan drew near, and as he listened, he realized that the voice was arguing with God. Yet Raan couldn't hear God's side of the discussion, only the flummoxed words of a desperate person lamenting. It felt embarrassing to eavesdrop on someone's prayers, so he distracted himself by leaning against the wall, checking to see if his fingernails needed biting, and fumbling with the stone in his pocket. The words, *wait and see*, popped into his mind, and he noticed his tension fading and his curiosity rising.

The voice stopped, and shuffling sounds came closer. Raan stood in dead silence behind the door as it slowly opened. Then a most unusual Bibgit crawled out of the coal chute and dusted himself off. Like all Bibgits, he had a broad face framed by long, jet-black curly hair, but he had extra-large sapphire eyes and was over five feet tall. Blue eyes were unheard of among Bibgits, and the tallest rarely topped five feet in height. He wore a gray bandana (or was it merely a dirty white one?) and had loose-fitting, grayish-brown pants, a yellow tunic, leather sandals, and a leather bag slung over his shoulder. In his right hand, he held a half-eaten carrot; in his left hand, he held a walking stick.

"A lovely morning we're having after the storm," said Raan with friendly sarcasm.

The startled person looked up, noticed Raan, and sprang away in a full sprint like a startled rabbit. Unfortunately, a downed tree branch sent him sprawling, slamming him face-down into the rocky grass. He didn't get up. Raan sped to the person's prone body and knelt beside it.

"Are you okay? Can you talk? What hurts?"

The figure moaned.

"So many questions," came a weak reply. "I don't know what's worse, this inquisition before breakfast or my broken arm," said the little man as he rolled over in agony, revealing a right arm that was bent at such a strange angle that it made Raan queasy.

The man struggled to sit up and yelped as his arm dangled limply.

"We'll have to immobilize it for now," said Raan, improvising a splint from a straight branch and some twine from his pocket. With his belt, he lashed the arm to the man's body and helped him to his feet, but the man cried out, "My knee!" Blood was seeping through his pant leg.

"Nothing for it; I'll have to carry you."

"Take your hands off me, I say!" said the man, trying to appear dignified.

But the stranger had no choice in the matter. So, with the man in his arms, Raan walked to the cottage, where Casy made the Bibgit comfortable. Later that day, the doctor set the arm correctly and examined the knee, which was only deeply bruised and cut when it scraped the fallen limb.

"He'll be fine in time, said the doctor. "Bibgits are quick healers, and I confess I have a little experience with them. They rarely get sick and are resilient beyond ordinary folks. They're quite tough in the fiber. Still, keep him quiet as long as you can."

[11]
Gerontius Boing

THAT NIGHT, THE FOURSOME enjoyed a pot of stew with fresh-baked bread and learned the Bibgits name was Gerontius Boing, but he liked to be called GB.

Seth began, "So now that we're all content with Casy's delicious meal, thank you, my dear." He nodded at Casy, and she made a little bow. "I'm curious how you came to be praying in the basement of the House of Hearing"."

Casy said, "First, how are you doing? Is the pain bad?"

"Thanks for asking; I can manage," said GB. "You have been so kind to make me comfortable. I never thought . . ." GB stopped himself.

The three sat staring, waiting for his next word. Reluctantly, GB said, blushing, "I never thought townspeople could be so kind. I've been hanging around for weeks, but you haven't noticed. Ever since the f" . . ." His voice trailed off cautiously.

The three looked at each other and then back at GB.

"Please don't be angry; I've been sleeping in the basement for some time."

"Ever since the fire?" asked Casy.

"I confess I took the liberty of making myself a guest in the hallowed house. But I haven't touched or taken anything holy except occasional scraps of bread leftover after a service; sometimes I get so hungry."

"I thought we had some well-fed holy mice," said Seth, causing GB to cover his mouth with his good hand and stare at the table, afraid to look up. "Don't worry I'm glad it went to a good cause. Where do you normally live?"

"I've stayed around town in different places for over a year," said GB. "The last place I lived was the barn that burned down. Some Bibgits accused me of starting the fire, but that's not true. Most of them shun me or whisper among themselves if they see me. In the market, they turn away and act like I don't exist, ignoring anything I say."

"That's awful." Casy scowled and clenched her fists. "Why would they treat you that way?"

"Well, mainly for two reasons. First, because I'm orphaned," said GB.

"Oh, I'm so sorry," said Casy. "What happened? If it's not too painful to tell."

GB's eyes clouded while he stared into space, then said, "Before I was born, my mom had a job as the Grand Protector's housekeeper. She served him for two years, but when she got pregnant with me, she was fired."

"And your dad?" Raan' asked.

"I never knew my dad and we never talked about it, but I know my mom was a good woman!" GB's voice rose indignantly as if a cruel label stapled across his forehead reawakened a gruesome pain.

No one spoke for a long time, until Casy said, "Was?"

"Yes," GB continued, "She's gone. When I got old enough, my mom told me that when she began to show with me, Barredoch dismissed her. No one would hire her, but somehow she got money and cared for me, loved me, and taught me to read, reason, and have faith. Last year, she died of fever.

None of the Bibgits would hire me, and they treated me like I had a disease. I picked up errands or little jobs for townspeople to earn a little here and there, but I couldn't make enough to pay for my own home, so I started staying with kindhearted folk who gave me a spare bed or pile of hay to sleep on in exchange for chores."

"But why wouldn't they hire and teach you a trade?" asked Casy.

"I was never offered the Okabe and welcomed into the moot," said GB, watching each of their faces.

Raan looked confused, and Casy listened politely, fiddling with the ties of her apron. Only Seth sat back knowingly.

They watched as GB settled in a little and adjusted his sore arm. "Every new moon, the Bibgit men and boys gather around a bonfire seated in a large circle. Every face glows with red light, and scores of eyes twinkle like stars come to Earth. On a table near the fire is a jug of strong liquor. It's called Okabe. If a man wants to honor someone, he walks to the jug, takes a drink, and then brings it to the person he wants to honor. The honored person drinks and turns to another person he wants to honor, or he returns the jug to the table. Likewise, when a man deems a boy or lad ready to join the other men in the working community, he brings the jug to that lad, and if the lad accepts, he drinks, and at that point, he is considered a man and welcomed into the moot. Usually, a boy's father would be the one to welcome his son. I waited year after year, but no man admitted to being my father, so I was not allowed to join the working community. Work is sacred to the Bibgits."

"That's ridiculous!" Casy bristled, thumping her crutch. "So, they will let you starve just because no one will invite you to get drunk in front of a crowd! I'll never understand men!"

"It's complicated," said Raan, scratching behind his ear.

Then Seth queried, "You said there were two reasons no one liked you."

"Yes." GB recomposed himself and spoke with a twinkle in his eye. "I talk with the Voice."

Casy and Raan looked puzzled; Seth's brow creased as he looked closer at the lad.

"I can guess what you're thinking: this guy is crazy," said GB. "I often talk to The Voice in prayers, and he speaks to me through His scriptures and wise teachers, but sometimes, in rare special moments, He allows me to talk *with* him." GB emphasized the word with.

After a long, awkward silence, Seth said, "It's been a busy day. We should get some sleep. GB, you can sleep in our spare bed. Do you feel comfortable enough?"

"After sleeping in a basement or on hay bales, this seems like heaven. I'll be okay. Thank you for your kindness and listening ears. I don't think I've ever told my story to anyone before. Besides the Voice, that is."

"Thanks, GB; we are honored by your trust," said Seth, stretching out to light a small candle from the tabletop taper.

Raan could see that the following weeks were like heaven for GB, as he was nursed back to health by Casy. He noticed GB loved to read and devoured anything he could find in the family library. Raan also noted that GB proved to have a remarkable memory and was soon quoting passages from the classics and the Book of the People of The Voice.

At the end of a month, GB looked better than ever. Awkwardly, he spoke to the family one night and said he planned to leave.

"But where will you go?" Casy asked.

Raan and Seth looked at each other, waiting for GB.

"Since my hideout in the hallowed house has been discovered, I'll need to trust the Voice for something else. I can make rounds at the colony and see if anyone has a place available, or perhaps I can find a farmer or elder who needs assistance in exchange for a place to stay. After a month of Casy's cooking, I feel as strong as an ox."

"You may be as strong as an ox, but you're also as dumb as one! What about staying with us?" said Raan.

"We've already discussed it," said Casy.

"You can help with the chores and the business," said Raan.

"Oh, no. You have already been too kind. Er, I could never ask." said GB.

"Why not ask?" said Seth. "Asking is good for the soul. A little humility cleanses the heart!"

So GB fit in nicely as the fourth member of the family.

[12]
A Hollowed-Out Heart

HOW MANY TIMES do I have to remind you? I need perfection, not this mockery of a clean window. What am I dealing with, woman? My own flesh and blood is a fool of a son, an imbecilic paddywomp clinging to his momma's apron," said the Grand Protector, more cranky than usual.

"He's only eight years old. Give him time," said his wife, pleading for her boy, who was cringing at his mother's bedside.

"Can you show me how, Dad? I know I can do it," said the boy, looking up at the towering man.

"Are you joking!" the Grand Protector roared, pushing his enormous waist out more than usual. "What would people think if they saw their leader cleaning windows? Once you start down that road, people will always expect it. I have more demanding things to think about."

"Then why must he do it?" asked the mother with a cough, wincing slightly as if expecting a harsh rebuke. The Grand Protector glared at his bedridden wife and raised his hand but got control of his temper and relented.

"The boy needs to develop character," said Barredoch, smoothing the front of his silk waist-coat.

"And you don't?" muttered the bed-bound woman so quietly no one could hear. A painful spasm shook her, and she sank back into her pillow, coughing.

"Here, Mother, have a sip," said the lad, raising a glass of water to her lips, but the Grand Protector grabbed the glass.

"Nonsense," he bellowed. "She doesn't need babying!" He walked to the window and slid it open, allowing the cold winter air in. "She just needs some fresh air to clear away the stuffiness. It'll do her good!" With barely a glance at his wife or son, Barredoch shouldered out of the room.

Koal stood on a chair and reached for the window. Using all his strength, he wrenched it closed. His mother lay pale amid creamy bedclothes, and the boy tried to comfort her, gently stroking her hand as best as an eight-year-old could. It was burning with fever.

***

It took six men a whole day to dig her grave in the frozen earth. Koal watched, rigid with grief. As each spade bit into the stubborn ground, a little of his heart was hollowed out until all that was left was a gaping hole.

Now, a decade later, Koal had one habit he was proud of. He would visit his mother's grave every week, whatever the weather, and bring a flower to lay on her headstone.

His tender memories of his mother didn't outshine the bitterness he carried about her death. But his father wouldn't talk about her. So Koal lived in a lonely world of feelings he couldn't talk about and distracted himself with dreams of power.

[13]
Warp and Weft

AMID TREES ABLAZE WITH AUTUMN colors, GB and Raan jogged through a mulberry grove to a neighboring village to deliver a part needed to repair a silk loom that had broken and injured the weaver.

"Thanks for coming, GB; I couldn't do this alone," said Raan.

"No problem, glad to help. I'm amazed when I think of all the folk it takes to make a bolt of mulberry silk or hand-knotted carpet. Everyone in the family has a job," said GB as they huffed along.

"Some harvest and some spin. Others weave, transport, and sell," said Raan.

"It's a *tightly knit, er, woven* community," said GB, unable to resist the pun.

Raan rolled his eyes. "They can create any pattern imaginable. And these families have handed down their secrets for generations. The art takes years to master."

"The cloth is beautiful, but something bothers me," said GB. "Look at their hands and how their backs curve because of the hours of bending over their work."

"Yes, those are the trademarks of the craft," said Raan. "To an insider, those marks are a badge of honor, like the calloused hands of a carpenter or the baggy eyes of a scholar."

"Or the calluses on Seth's knees from praying through the years," said GB, chuckling.

Raan didn't know why GB's remark about prayer annoyed him, but he ignored it and said, "I've never seen any Bibgits working in the silk trade. Where do Bibgits work? No one's ever mentioned it."

"That's because it's secret," said GB.

The two lads were silent after they finished the work on the loom. Raan thought about the mission he'd been sent to do and worried that the men in the music shop had chosen the wrong guy.

[14]
WAR AT THE DAWN OF TIME

IT WAS MIDMORNING WHEN the lads left the weavers', and GB led them in a direction Raan had never been.

"You have to promise me never to tell anyone about this place I'm showing you," said GB in a hushed tone.

"Okay, I promise. Where are we going?"

"You have to trust me, but the adventure comes with a price."

"Price? What price?" said Raan. "What's the catch?"

"No more than you can afford. Just let me tell you a story I've been working on. It's like a myth, but better."

"Long hikes are made for mythical tales. The more magical, the better." Raan stopped a moment to adjust his pack and looked into the cloudless sky. As he touched the stone in his pocket, a quiet voice in his mind said, "Come, I've got something to show you." His curiosity roused, Raan bounded after his friend.

"Before history, there was a mighty spirit being," GB began. "It was the source of all flow. It was the single point where peace and energy became one—part life giver, part inspiration, part healer, and part counselor. It was pure thought, total compassion, a living Word that had the power to create merely by speaking anything from Its imagination. It called Itself Iam."

That's a strange name. It sounds more like a declaration: I'm real, thought Raan as he caught up to the limber Bibgit.

"Iam's favorite thing was to create. He made galaxies, black holes, billions of stars, and numerous spirit beings in the deep heavens. He created them because he loved them. Like a painter loves his painting or a writer loves his story, He loved making them, caring for them, and helping them become beautiful," said GB with a gleam in his eye. "He loved seeing them delight in each other and all His gifts."

"You mean," said Raan, "like a cook enjoying a table full of hungry guests delighting in a meal he worked hard to prepare?"

"That's the idea!" said GB as he continued:

"Iam gave the spirit beings many gifts like fun, imagination, laughter, music, and honor. But he didn't want slaves; he wanted friends, so He gave them the best gift of all: freedom. Most spirit beings used their freedom to do marvelous things to honor Iam and each other, but some wanted honor for themselves, and they grew worried about losing the honor they had."

GB paused his tale for a moment to navigate a bit of tricky terrain. Raan followed GB as he ducked under a low branch and passed into a grove of hawthorns flush with ripe berries. The sun was warm, and the scents of wildflowers and fallen leaves reminded him of all that he loved about autumn. Bulbuls sang, and their scurries, flutters, chirps, and chatters filled the air. Still, since there was no trail, Raan wondered where they were going. Also, he was puzzled by an earthy, sweet, ripe fragrance he couldn't place.

"Where are you leading me?" asked Raan, too impatient to wait for GB's surprise.

"You'll see," said GB, looking back over his shoulder mischievously.

The two friends passed into a clearing overlooking a lush valley flanked by steep canyon walls that barred their path. A fast river cut through the gorge, sending sparkling spray into the sunshine. Raan imagined he was looking into the primordial depths of time, witnessing, in an inaugural act of creation, as the father of rivers carved the land in a thousand thousand variations springing from an imagination beyond mortal thought. A dragonfly buzzed near his face, and Raan was jogged back to the present.

"We cross up there," said GB eagerly as he pointed to a spot high up where a huge fallen tree trunk spanned the canyon above an energetic waterfall.

"There? Are you sure about this?" asked Raan dubiously.

GB shot back a glare that could have permanently frozen any waterfall. So, with the spray from the falling river misting his face, Raan followed his guide as he zigzagged up the slope.

"So what happens next?" Raan asked. "In the story, I mean."

GB took a deep breath and continued:

"Iam spoke, and a world appeared in deep heaven, and in that world, He set in motion the winds and oceans; he made plants, animals, and the cycles of life. And the spirit beings delighted in the new wonder, praised Iam, and worshiped Him. Yet some spirit beings were jealous and wanted to learn the secret of making worlds to get praise for themselves."

"Look! Over there . . . in the clearing," Raan whispered as a doe and two fawns perked their ears at the lads' approach.

Raan and GB froze, admiring the graceful creatures. Then, as if a spell had lifted, the deer effortlessly disappeared into a stand of junipers, flipping white tails in farewell, and the friends continued plodding upward.

One hundred yards further, they stumbled upon a ghastly mess and the remains of what looked like a sheep scattered amid the scrub oaks and thorns. It was fresh.

"What animal did this?" said Raan, noticing the swarming flies.

"Whatever it was it had to be big to drag a sheep all the way up here"," said GB, gulping.

The lads trekked on, wary of every rustle, and searching for movement in the thickets.

"Iam made people," GB continued, quietly in case something was lurking nearby, "gave them many gifts, and made them the world's rulers. Iam also gave them the right to become His children if they wanted, children He'd love and cherish forever. Most of the spirit beings rejoiced at the plan, but others became upset, which was the reason for the war."

"War?" said Raan breathlessly, squeezing himself between a boulder and an oak tree.

"Yes, a terrible war. Some spirit beings didn't like that people could become Iam's children. They wanted to rule the people and be worshiped by them. After much debate in deep heaven, a third of the spirit beings chose to fight against Iam. Finally, after many battles and heroic deeds, the rebels were defeated, and as punishment, they were bound to the world. There, the rebels made mischief and corrupted its people. Yet some of the people resisted the mischief makers. They became a rebellion against the rebellion, choosing to follow Iam, loving him and each other as well as they could amid the chaos."

The two friends emerged at the top of the waterfall and stopped with the plunging water roaring in their ears, and GB stared into the mist. Raan waited to see if more of his tale was forthcoming, but GB remained silent and thoughtful.

"You said you've been working on that story," said Raan, unshouldering his pack and stretching, "but it sounds familiar. Did you make it up?"

"Well, not exactly. It's based on an old story that many believe. I only changed some of the terms and phrases, but hopefully none of the meaning."

"It sounds interesting when you tell it that way," offered Raan, "Do you think it's true?"

"As far as it goes, I do, but there is much more to the tale."

[15]

Deadly Crossing

THE GUYS LOOKED OUT over the canyon as the windswept mist teased their faces. The constant roar overwhelmed them as the river disappeared over the edge. For Raan, the sight was eerie. He was awed by the endless flow and the thundering power released as the water plummeted into the canyon below. Strangely, he felt compelled to imagine himself jumping into the swift current and free-falling in its torrent, whisked away like a leaf in a flood. Frightened by the strange temptation, Raan stepped back a couple of paces.

"This is our bridge!" shouted GB as he walked to one side of the hefty tree trunk spanning the river and clambered on. In twenty quick steps, he looked back from the opposite bank and beckoned Raan to follow.

"Give me a minute," shouted Raan. He wondered if there was any way out of this stunt other than shame or death. Death is more likely, he mused, thinking about Casy and Seth and the villagers. And of course, the mission. He wondered if there was an afterlife in this world or if, after a tragic fall, he would wake up in his Manhattan apartment. Thoughts of his comfortable pillow and the corner deli's giant meatball sandwich pulled at his mind, but he didn't plan on dying just yet. So after a deep breath, he touched the stone, and his courage awoke as he faced the log bridge.

"Stay to the center and look straight ahead!" called GB.

"Okay, okay," said Raan, fiddling with the straps of his rucksack. "I just gotta get balanced before I try," he lied. He was terrified of heights but too proud to admit it.

The river drummed endlessly between the stone cliffs, hissing in defiance of boulders and tree trunks piled along its banks.

GB yelled to his friend, "Just do it! You got this, bro!" not realizing Raan's inner struggle.

"Just gotta stay balanced," Raan assured himself as he scrambled onto the log, its coating of mossy slime oozing through his fingers. He stepped out over the canyon, shakily moving across the log, saying, "I got this, I got this."

About halfway, he got a little cocky, a balanced on one foot with his arms flapping like a bird. He tried hopping over a large knot, and the trick turned disastrous as he slipped and ended up splayed across the log on his belly, legs on one side, head and arms on the other. Rushing water thundered below.

"Raan!" GB howled with laughter but quickly sobered when he realized Raan was in trouble. "I'm coming to you!" he yelled.

"Wait, no, no, I can do this! Hold on!" Raan cried. For the moment, he became surprisingly calm; he was balanced, so he took time to focus with slow, steady breathing. Reaching his right arm under the log, he gripped his left pant leg. This gave him the balance to lift his right leg up and over the top of the log. Then, he eased his left shoulder over, and by locking his hands and hooking his feet together, he straddled the log, but now, he was backward, with his backside facing GB and the far bank. A fine sight I must look; I'll never make fun of a tree hugger again, thought Raan, his limbs wrapped tight around the precarious bridge.

"I see you're putting your best side forward," GB called with a laugh, his helpful attitude disappearing once the immediate danger was past.

In this awkward position, Raan began inching toward GB, who was laughing hysterically. But GB's mirth turned into a shout of terror when Raan's body began to slip to one side. Schaloop! He slid around until he was completely upside-down, dangling like a sloth above the raging waterfall. Miraculously, he held on, ignoring the pain in his arms and legs, and slowly wormed along the bottom of the log until his rump met solid ground. With GB's help, Raan scrabbled onto the far bank.

Once his friend was safe, GB said, "I hope you're not planning to audition for the circus soon. We'd hate to lose you. You'd make a terrific acrobatic clown."

"Nope, I save that job for you, and you won't need any makeup," said Raan, relieved to be rubbing sore arms.

They plopped down on the grass and rested, gazing up at the clear sky. Coming so close to death gives a person a wonderful appetite, so they pulled out the food they'd packed and ate lunch. Soon, the pulsing roar of the water lost its terror, and the two resumed their trek.

After about half an hour of steep climbing, GB said, "Now I need to blindfold you."

"You must be kidding. What for?" said Raan, who'd had about as much humiliation as he could take for one day.

"You'll see—and you won't see," said GB with a grin, ignoring Raan's flustered state. He pulled a dark bandana from his pocket and bound Raan's eyes. "Now, I'll lead you for a little while, not long."

"I'll expect payback for every stubbed toe," said Raan.

"There'll be no need," spoke the steady voice of GB, picking out a path through the pinewoods as they neared their secret destination.

[16]
THE FORBIDDEN VALLEY

BECAUSE HE WAS BLINDFOLDED, Raan sensed things differently, like the cool air on his face and the tickle of sweat trailing down his neck. He heard sounds he hadn't noticed before, and the fresh, fruity fragrance he couldn't place earlier became so strong he couldn't smell anything else. Finally, they stopped, and GB removed the blindfold. Raan staggered at what he saw.

"Here we are," said GB, taking a deep breath.

They stood on a high, rocky outcropping overlooking the top hills, which rolled in perfect curves, like floating islands in an undulating sea of trees. Alternating emerald and brown stripes as far as the eye could see, dazzling patchworks of brilliant red, violet, blue, and gold, bordered by mists that caressed each garden in pillows of white.

Raan thought it looked like a surrealistic mountain-top garden spanning the hilltops. Finally, Raan staggered, overwhelmed by the beauty of sight and scent. "It's a paradise, more beautiful than anything I've ever seen."

"These are the forbidden gardens. The King entrusted them to the Bibgits generations ago, and the prince has watched over them for as long as anyone can remember."

Raan strained his eyes, trying to see what the stunning colors were made of. Partly due to the sweet smell, he guessed they must be flowers—hundreds of thousands of blossoms covering the mountaintops.

"The Bibgits are the gatherers and gardeners of the land's most fragrant flowers, medicinal plants, and luscious grapes. We prune, cultivate, harvest, distill, and press for the perfumers, healers, and wineries," boasted GB. "We've protected them for hundreds of years. It's death to come uninvited."

"It looks like an artist's work," said Raan, wishing he had a camera. "It looks so healthy and lush."

"That's because skilled, tender hands prune away all but the most fruitful. Season by season, we guide their growth to produce the choicest of everything."

Raan shaded his eyes and looked out over the stunning landscape, trying to take everything in. Breezes from one direction brought him scents of rich herbs, such as lavender, chamomile, and sage. From another point of the compass came rose, coriander, and mint, mingled with the fragrance of grapevines. He noticed tiny figures passing among the fields—pack animals hauling carts and many people intent on their work.

GB spoke again, "Night harvests produce the most flavorful fruit, so tonight at midnight by torchlight, hundreds of harvesters will begin to select and gently pick the grape clusters. Others carry them to the winery, where they are pressed by the feet of an army of dancers and become the best juice and wine. On other days, they harvest the herbs and flowers. Everyone shares in the labor, and all share in the fruit of the fruit."

Raan paused in thought, curious about GB's last phrase. Finally, he asked, "What do you mean by the fruit of the fruit?"

GB laughed, "Its fragrance is all around us, but not how you imagine. It's on the mountaintop, in the valley, through the forest, and in your home. It's among friends and even with you in hard times. I can taste it now."

"Do you mean the smell of the gardens?" asked Raan.

GB put his hands behind his back, poised himself as if he were going to give a speech:

-You can see it in the face of harvesters.
In the smiles of kings and commoners,
In the eyes of brides and grooms,
In the songs of wedding tunes.
As they eat and drink and laugh and pray,
They receive it gladly and give it away!

GB grinned, proud of the riddling rhyme he had made up on the spot.

"Okay," said Raan, accepting GB's unspoken challenge. "Let me guess: fun."

"Nope."

"Delight."

"Good guess, but nope."

"Cheerfulness!"

"Guess again," said GB, becoming pleased with himself.

"Excitement,"

"Nice try."

"Compassion, good manners, clean teeth . . . I don't know; I give up!" shouted Raan.

"Okay, alright, if you twist my arm, it's the fruit of joy. Joy is all around you. Its breezes touch our faces and tease our senses. It's in the air, ready to refresh. Like a fruit that's available, ripe for picking."

"Joy?" questioned Raan. "Are you kidding? I've seen too many unhappy people to believe happiness or joy is all around."

"Sadly, there are too many unhappy people, but I'm not talking about happiness; I'm talking about the joy of belonging, being part of something outside yourself."

Raan wondered about GB's last comment but didn't say anything. The friends stood silently thinking, watching the glowing gardens in the magical light of late afternoon.

"Someday, I'll take you for a closer view, but we need to go; it'll get dark soon. I know a shortcut."

GB led Raan along the cliff's edge when suddenly, Raan felt something whiz past his head, close to his ear. Then another whooshed past his arm, and another overhead.

"Arrows! Get down!" he cried. "Someone's shooting at us!"

[17]
LANDSLIDE

AS THEY LAY FLAT ON THE GROUND, GB risked lifting his head to look. "It's my people!" yelled GB, jumping up and waving his arms frantically, calling in the Bibgit language, "Shailo! Shailo! Kara munzie!" Stop! Stop! We're friends!

Raan stayed low, marveling at GB's boldness. Standing proud and alert, GB was an easy target. The shooting stopped, and four grim-looking Bibgit men on either side of them appeared from the forest. They held longbows and carried hunting knives. They cautiously approached the friends with arrows nocked.

"You!" said a man taller than the others. "Fatherless wanderer, how dare you come here? And with an outsider!"

The two locked eyes, but GB remained silent, making a statement with his unflinching gaze. The man turned his attention to Raan, who had now risen in support of his friend.

The Bibgit's eyes narrowed. "I know you!" said the man surveying Raan. "I've seen you before! Take off your shirt!" he commanded as the others bent their bows.

This would be the perfect time for a trip back to Manhattan, thought Raan, and, not wanting to become a pincushion just then, he removed his sweat-soaked shirt, revealing the scars he'd received from burns during the fire. The archers lowered their weapons.

"I knew it!" said the man, compassion flooding his eyes. "You saved my sister's children from the fire."

Raan's eyes burned with dry tears as he remembered that night. He recalled the soot-covered faces of those little ones clinging to their mother and asked, "Are they well?"

"Yes, well and thriving. They are there," said the man, pointing to the gardens.

"It gives me . . . joy to know they are safe," said Raan formally, remembering GB's conversation a few minutes ago.

The archers all looked at each other, then whispered together. Raan looked at the ground. Finally the tall Bibgit said, "I'm called Kia, and I pronounce you a friend of the Bibgit nation!" Kia took a flask from his side, took a sip, and handed it to Raan.

Taking the vessel, Raan took a sip of the strong drink, saying, "I'm called Raan, and I accept the honor of your fellowship with joy!"

The four Bibgit sentries broke into a song, and Raan and GB stood in respectful amazement until they ended.

Again, Kia spoke: "How is it, Bibgit friend, that you are found with this fatherless one? His kind is an abomination to our people."

Raan fumbled with the white stone in his pocket, unsure of how to respond and thinking, I could really use some wisdom right now. Suddenly, words popped into his mind, and he heard himself say, "No man is fatherless. And this one, has a Father in heaven who is above us all. I honor him because of his glorious Father and his deep faith in the one who walks unseen!" Raan had no idea where these words came from and waited to see what would happen.

The Bibgit archers whispered among themselves for several minutes. GB and Raan remained motionless but calm, not daring to say anything.

The Bibgit men finished their conversation and faced Raan and GB. "Whoo I ka Pa tee!" Then let it be so! Kia passed the flask to GB. "Let this man who is a son of the unseen heavenly Father be welcomed as a Bibgit man forever!"

GB took the flask, looked at it, paused, and then looked to heaven and said, "I accept this friendship and its honor because of the Father of us all." He sipped the drink and almost threw up because it was so strong, but he kept his dignity and swallowed. Afterward, he sighed and looked to heaven.

The men sang their song again, said farewell, and disappeared into the woods. GB was nearly walking on air. He led Raan silently for a long time along the gorge's edge. The sun sank low, the shadows deepened, and the landscape glowed with miraculous golden light.

Stepping out onto a rocky ledge, Raan pointed. "I can see the roadway down the gorge in the trees."

Eager to end their journey, the lads quickened their pace, but a thunderous roar shook the hilltop, and they stared at each other in wide-eyed amazement! The entire hillside seemed to be moving;

trees, rocks, and the grassy ledge began to slide toward the valley below.

GB cried out, "Help!" his voice was drowned in the din of the landslide.

Raan's eyes darted from side to side. He grabbed his friend and leaped onto a large flat boulder just as the ground slipped away under them. They looked like a couple of frantic cartoon characters surfing the landslide, riding on the rock, their faces frozen in a mix of terror and delight.

"I can't see!" croaked Raan as the dust and debris surrounded them in an impenetrable cloud. Gasping and coughing, the lads balanced on the precarious rock until the sliding hillside became still near the bottom of the valley.

"Wait! It's not done!" yelled GB, grabbing Raan as he started to jump off. In a flash, an enormous flood of loose gravel broke above them, engulfing their rock perch and almost sweeping them away.

"That last slide would have buried me alive! Thanks, my friend!"

GB nodded and looked down at the field of smoking rubble.

"That was some shortcut," said Raan, brushing dirt from his clothes. "Look! There's the road." Raan shot a sideways glance at his dust-covered friend and noticed GB standing with an air of quiet confidence in the wake of near death. *Humility with boldness*, thought Raan. *The pruner's knife has made him strong.*

If you dwell in the eternal, there is no time, neither forward nor backward, only a satisfied present because eternal satisfaction rests solely in the heavenly Kingdom and not in your worldly accomplishments.

(From The Journals of Zambo the Mute)

[18]

A GILDED LETTER

MONTHS LATER, A COMMOTION broke out in town that caused Raan to smile. Two strangers from the country drove into town on a gigantic wagon overflowing with fresh fruits and vegetables to sell at the market. One was tall, with a bushy beard, and the other was broad, sporting a big mustache.

They had baskets of apples redder and juicier than anyone had ever seen; there were oranges, melons, and luscious vegetables that made your mouth water. The local produce paled in comparison, so the townspeople flocked to the wagon to buy from the strangers.

Seeing their day's profits gone due to the newcomer's competition, the local merchants grumbled, and their complaints reached the Grand Protector. Seizing the opportunity to parade his own importance, Barredoch swaggered into the crowded market and directly to the newcomers' wagon, shouting, "What's all this!"

Many people ignored him, but when the Grand Protector raised his right hand, several rough-looking Qerds stepped up beside him. Most people quickly moved away from the stranger's cart, leaving the two men alone with Raan, standing next to their almost empty cart.

At first, no one spoke, but the man with the bushy beard broke the silence with the heartiest welcome anyone could imagine. "It's so good to see you! Thank you for coming! You must be the Grand Protector."

"Your visit honors us," said the other. "We've heard so much about you."

"Rarely do we have the privilege of serving so distinguished a customer. We regret we have so little left," said the first man, gesturing toward the nearly empty wagon.

Barredoch took a deep breath as if he were about to make a grand proclamation but was interrupted by the man with the mustache: "We've kept something special just for you." He pulled a basket from under the driver's bench and announced, "A score of ripe figs, and a dozen morel mushrooms, a rare delight."

The Grand Protector looked skeptically at the exotic mushrooms, but his eyes lit up at the sight of the ripe figs—his favorite. The men presented the gift basket to Barredoch, and his tension eased. The Qerds relaxed.

Recovering his dignity, the Grand Protector said, "Our humble market is greatly honored to welcome two such traveling merchants."

"No great honor at all," said the first man.

"We enjoy sharing the fruit of our gardens. It's our privilege," said the second.

The Grand Protector was taken aback by such courtesy from merchants. But stammering, he recovered. "Then you must stay and enjoy our town's humble hospitality."

"Regrettably, we must be moving on. First, we are to deliver this letter from his highness Prince Terrion."

Barredoch's face brightened, and he approached the man holding an official-looking envelope. But the man turned instead to Raan, who recognized him as one of the men from the Village Musical Instrument Emporium. Raan took the envelope and smiled, brimming with questions.

"Regrettably, we must leave to attend to an important matter across the mountain," said the man with the mustache as he winked at Raan.

"But you just arrived," insisted Raan. "At least stay and have lunch. Casy makes the best candied walnuts, and her koluchka are to die for."

After a nod to the crestfallen Raan and a bow to the Grand Protector, the men drove off, leaving the Grand Protector and Raan standing face to face.

"Aren't you going to open it?" said the Grand Protector.

"I think I'll take it home and open it there."

"Preposterous!" said the Grand Protector, quickly snatching the envelope from the lad. "The community leader should be the first to see such important documents. He greedily broke its wax seal and removed a sheet of parchment. After a few seconds, he said, "This is gibberish! The prince must be out of his mind!" Unable to contain his delight.

With contempt, the Grand Protector tossed the letter in the air, but Raan snatched it before it hit the ground and puzzled over what he read:

After a moldy dinner of cucumber pie, I barely ate anything. For years, I danced, but am now singing, being thrilled and held by my captive imagination. And in deepest consideration, my dream butterfly castle rises, so come what may at day's end, once we get there, yesterday's pigeons are ripe. For three days, imaginary dangers tickle us, trust every time the Badger's polishing stone makes sharp the sword blade end. Everyone that draws his shoe near majesty finds in the effort haste brings about the gold of kings. To watch faithful friends cry servant serve fairyland Z A M

[19] CANDLES AND CODES

THAT NIGHT, RAAN SHOWED the letter to Seth, Casy, and GB, who read it over and over, thinking it might be a riddle, but nobody could figure it out.

"Do you think the prince is out of his mind like Barredoch thinks?" Said Casy, whose puzzle-solving muscles were beginning to wane.

A blank stare from GB didn't help, and Raan reread the lines slowly, hoping for a new revelation, but nothing new came to him.

Finally, as their candle became a tiny stub, the older man's face brightened.

"Of course, it's a code!" Exclaimed Seth, rolling up his sleeves, "Get another candle!"

Four sets of bright eyes stared at the parchment in the flickering light. Reading the note backward was just as confusing. They tried every other word and got more gibberish.

With feverish excitement, they tried different combinations of word order without results until, after much futile guessing, the family began to look a bit glum. Finally, Seth examined the envelope and became animated.

“There’s something else here! It may be a clue! Taking a sharp knife, he carefully slid the blade into the seams of the envelope so that it came apart, and there, to everyone’s surprise, they saw the drawing of a map, many pictograms, and a row of symbols. There were no names, but there were several clear landmarks and a maze containing a dotted line that ended in a spot shaped like a diamond.

“Maybe the diamond marks where Terrion’s treasure is hidden,” said Casy.

“Perhaps,” said her dad, “but I wonder what this string of characters means?” He pointed to a row of symbols in a corner. ⍈10X⍗10⇸3|2X2=Go.

“We know it must mean something or it wouldn’t be written here,” said GB.

“But what?” Asked Casy, trying to hide her frustration.

"Knowing that there is an answer is half the battle in discovering the solution to any puzzle," said Seth, as much to keep his own spirits alive as anyone else's.

"Wait!" Cried Raan, grasping the stone in his pocket. "Let me have a clean parchment!" He remembered reading something like this in a spy novel back home.

Raan drew a crude ten-by-ten checkerboard on the white sheet. "Ten boxes across, ten down, gauging by the arrows in the symbol string. Now write the message in the boxes, one word in each box."

"What does the 3 mean?" Asked Casy.

"Maybe, three to the right, because of the crossover arrow pointing right."

"Let's see," said Raan as he wrote the words from the message in each box, starting in the top left corner. They checked every third word and ended with gibberish again.

"What does the 2 X 2 mean? Could it be a starting point?" Said Casy.

Then, starting two boxes down and two boxes across, Raan circled every third word, and they all gasped. The circled words formed the message:

I am being held captive in my
castle. Come at once. There are
three dangers. Trust the stone.

The end draws near. In haste,
the king's faithful servant, Z.

[20]
THE STONE REVEALED

GB WAS THE FIRST TO SPEAK, "The Prince is in trouble; that's clear enough."

"But what are the three dangers?" asked Casy.

"What about the stone? Did we get that right?" said GB

"I wonder," said Seth. "There are several mysteries here."

As if drawn by a magnet, all three turned to Raan, whose face blushed.

"I can help with the last mystery," said Raan, drawing the white stone from his pocket. "This must be the stone in the message."

The three looked at the jewel-like rock and the strange markings on it.

"May I look at it?" asked Seth.

Raan felt a strange reluctance to give it up, but he nodded and handed the white stone to Seth, who examined it closely and then gave it back.

"I've never seen the likes of this before. The markings are curious; I'm sure they have meaning, but they're not a language that I'm familiar with. How long have you had this?"

"I found it the first da . . ." he paused and continued, "On the day of the regatta, in the woods near the hay fields."

"But what is there about the stone that we are supposed to trust? I don't get it," asked Casy, who was speaking the thoughts of the others.

Again, all eyes were fixed on Raan, who cleared his throat. "This is hard to explain, and likely you'll think I'm bonkers, but ever since I've had the stone, words of wisdom and courage have come to me that are unusual and inspiring. Thoughts come to me whenever I touch the stone or think about it in times of need. I don't understand how, but they do."

The others just stared at Raan, who thought, I can really use some wisdom now.

"Remember the fire? The archers at the hidden garden? And there was the older woman, Emma, the stone gave me compassion for her I wouldn't have had on my own. Just now, when we cracked the code, the stone gave me insight I couldn't have had on my own. And other times when I've been lonely or confused, words of comfort come into my mind when I touch the stone," said Raan. "I've no idea why or how, but it's true."

"You have been different lately, but I thought that might be . . ." Casy paused.

"Might be what?" asked GB.

"Nothing, really. Forget it!" said Casy, straightening her apron and looking away.

The older man scanned Raan quizzically and then returned to the message.

"I agree with GB," remarked Seth, "The prince is undoubtedly in trouble and needed to send the message in code so unfriendly eyes wouldn't see. But why did he send it to you Raan?"

"I'm not sure," said Raan trying to avoid eye contact. "I think I've seen the two men before."

"Intriguing, I wonder . . ." said Seth before he was interrupted by GB.

"What about the secret map?"

"Yes, the map. It must be that Prince Terrion fears for his life and didn't want the secret of his treasure to fall into the wrong hands," exclaimed Seth.

"That's it!" the young people agreed.

"But what about the three dangers?" asked Casy. "What could they be?"

"It's late. Have mercy on an old soul," said the holy listener-handyman, whose weariness was noticeably getting the better of him. "Let's sleep on it and pray for wisdom. The morning may bring fresh ideas."

They went to bed, and as the house became quiet, night sounds filtered in through a half-open window. The older man's steady, quiet breathing could be heard as he slumbered in the deep rest of faith. Raan couldn't get comfortable. He fussed with his pillow, twisted to one side, then the other; bent legs, straight legs; no matter what position he took, his arms always seemed to get in the way. Finally, he sat upright and confronted the question bugging him: How did Prince Terrion know about the white stone?

All the events seemed random, but Raan realized that many things were connected in ways he didn't understand. He now knew his mission was to rescue the prince, while at the same time foiling the plot of Barredoch and the silk merchants and perhaps improving the quality of life for the people. But he wasn't any closer to knowing what he should do. He tried touching the stone, and all he heard were the words, "Patience is a fruit of the Spirit," but that wasn't helpful. In his mind he replayed all the events that had happened since his journey began and concluded that strange things were going on he couldn't see—yet.

His uncertainty about his situation led him to recount all the bungles, mistakes, and botched encounters in his New York life, which triggered a longing for all his favorite foods. He finally started to doze, thinking of Coney dogs and potato chips as an amber glow began to creep up from behind the eastern mountains.

[21]
THREE DANGERS

THE FOLLOWING DAY, Raan awoke late, feeling he had hardly slept. The sun was bright, and he could hear Casy moving around and GB humming outside. Seth was already out running errands. The morning promised to be as beautiful as ever, but Raan's thoughts were already spinning.

"Morning, Casy. How'd you sleep?" said Raan as he climbed out of his loft.

"Not much," said Casy, setting the breakfast table.

A single braid lay over one shoulder as she placed bowls and spoons in four places and set a steaming loaf on the table.

"All's ready," she announced. "Can you call GB to bring in the milk and some butter from the cold cellar?"

The three were just sitting down when Seth came in.

"What a gorgeous morning! I'm starving! It smells delicious; you didn't have to wait for me."

"You always seem to arrive just in time for a meal," teased Casy, passing him the fresh bread, raspberry jam, goat cheese, and her famous candied walnuts.

"I've been in town investigating and have learned something interesting. The woodcutters say that for the last six months, a lot of livestock have disappeared. Men have found remains in the deep woods that suggest that a large hunting animal, or pack, has come to the mountain. They said that they placed traps and pits in the high forest, hoping to snare the beast, but so far, they have had no luck. This could be one of the dangers mentioned in the note."

Raan sipped his milk, intently focused on Seth, and added, "GB and I saw the remains of a fresh carcass of a sheep high up in the woods near the waterfall. It looked as if a large hunting animal had ravaged it."

"What if it's a Chimera?" GB asked.

"There's no such thing as a Chimera. They're only bogey animals from kids' fairytales. Aren't they?" said Casy with an eye on Seth.

"It's hard to say, sometimes myths have their basis in history. I've never seen one," said Seth as he looked into his cup of tea.

Raan unconsciously touched the outside of his pocket to feel the stone, and an image of a bird-faced tiger with a serpent's tail flashed into his mind. He shuddered and looked across the room at the hand axe hanging on the wall.

Seth broke the silence: "I also learned from the storekeeper that Barredoch and the Qerds had a closed meeting last night and are spreading a rumor that Raan and I are involved in a plot against the prince. Nothing else was said, but I'm guessing Barredoch's rumors could be the second danger. I don't know if the rumors will mean any more than we'll get scowls from the gullible, but time will tell."

"That's ridiculous!" said Casy, pushing her chair away from the table. "How dare they say such things! Was Koal involved?"

"As far as I know, Koal wasn't there. I think he's been away from town for weeks; I don't know where."

"Probably at one of the waterfront guest houses, living it up," said GB.

"Let's not start rumors on our end," said Seth. "We've enough to think about figuring out our riddles and what to do regarding the message. As far as the third danger is concerned, I'm drawing a blank."

"Maybe it has something to do with one of us?" said Casy, whose intuition usually proved reliable.

"Maybe so, but we don't know anything certain. Let's keep our eyes and ears open and learn what we can. Meanwhile, let's figure out how to help Prince Terrion."

[22] SKIN'S WATERPROOF

THE FOURSOME AGREED that someone should go to the Prince's castle immediately. Raan was elected, since his long legs and wiry frame made him the obvious choice to cut cross-country with speed, following a route GB knew would avoid the winding road and save several days. Raan planned to start before dawn and travel mountain paths to avoid unfriendly eyes.

He tied the stone to a silk string and wore it under his shirt to keep it safe, feeling sure his mission was finally taking shape. Still, he was unsure what to do with the corrupt silk merchants and the people's harsh working conditions. He would just have to trust the stone and believe he'd know what to do when the time came.

The chill mist on Raan's face accelerated his sense of adventure as he set out by the last light of the moon. It was quiet, and he was far from home when the day dawned. Excited to be on his way, Raan pumped forward briskly, but his enthusiasm wavered when a fine rain began to fall. Dauntless, Raan plodded on, proclaiming to the clouds, "Skin's waterproof."

By noon, the sprinkle had become a downpour, and Raan took shelter under a gigantic oak. The relentless dripping made him think of all the time he was losing, and waiting annoyed him so much that walking in the steady rain seemed more bearable. So he slogged through the showers, listening to the glop-glop of his soggy feet in soaking boots. He watched the raindrops fall from the brim of his hat hoping for a hot drink when he reached the castle and wondered if this trip was such a good idea.

He thought of Manhattan and figured it would be midwinter by then. But remembering the icy blasts of wind cutting through the streets, mounting piles of snow, and stacks of uncollected garbage made a little rain seem tolerable. He smiled and thought, That's what makes New Yorkers so tough. They can handle anything. With that attitude, he plodded on.

Before long, the sun returned, igniting the landscape in a glistening dazzle of pools and shimmering leaves. But footing was treacherous, as the path crossed many slippery roots and rocks. By afternoon, his progress took him to a tree-lined lake that marked the beginning of gray-green slopes leading to the high country.

Using a map made by GB, he pressed on, scrambling a lot on the steep hillside, gripping stumps and branches to keep from sliding into the forest below.

Eventually GB's map led him along the edge of a deep canyon. A swollen river thundered a hundred feet below, cascading in roaring power. Its brown foam made him think about root beer and street vendors selling slushies at home. He never thought he'd long for the smell of exhaust fumes, the harsh metallic screech of a braking subway, or the taste of fresh salami on a little Italy hero, but it's hard to predict what the sight of a root beer river might inspire.

He made quick work of the many rills and streams with long jumps, and in one case, he used a long, straight branch as a pole and vaulted across. He narrowly missed falling into a cleverly hidden pit that was at least ten feet deep and as many wide and across.

He planned to follow the canyon for several miles until he reached the road leading to the castle road bridge; he figured he'd be there by twilight.

Just then, he saw a flash of white moving in the rocks about a quarter mile behind him. He waited in the shadow of two trees and thought he saw something moving amid the boulders. Could it be a trick of the light? He couldn't see clearly what was following him, so he continued along the edge, moving more quickly.

[23]
HUNTED

AN HOUR PASSED, AND RAAN climbed around and over boulders, through debris, all along the canyon edge. Every so often, he'd look over his shoulder to try to glimpse something he thought was following him, but he never saw anything clearly.

Desperately, Raan moved quickly, keeping under cover and avoiding the exposed cliff top and open areas. When he saw nothing behind him, he moved, glancing back often and running when he could. From the dark eves of the trees, he looked back and saw a snake-like tail vanish behind a rock, and his blood froze. It was gaining on him.

Gripping the stone hanging from his neck, he prayed and searched for a way across the canyon. There was no bridge and no way to climb down.

Scrambling again, he noticed a straight, thin pine tree growing beside the cliff's edge. At that point, the gorge was narrow. Would the tree span the distance? He wondered. Can it hold me? No other options. The logic was cold and deadly. Feverishly, he attacked the tree with his hand axe, cutting away the lower branches, and hewing the trunk in just the right spot so it would fall across the gorge. Just as he made the final stroke, the beast appeared. The tree fell, but Raan didn't notice.

Nothing could have prepared him for this moment. A massive head like an owl, as big as Raan's chest, appeared from the undergrowth, followed by its muscular feline body of an albino tiger. Milky white with black stripes, the Chimera stood as still as ice, assessing its prey. It bared yellow fangs in a razor-sharp beak and resonated with a low-pitched growl that rose to an ear-piercing screech!

Raan stood as tall as he could and lifted both hands in the air, waving the axe and yelling nonsense words: "An Eee Ya! Kamboole Aa! Polli. Polli, polli, nswee pagoo!"

"What's that supposed to mean?" Raan muttered under his breath, planting his feet, ready to leap over the edge, preferring to die on the rocks below rather than be mauled and eaten.

The Chimera looked confused for a moment, but soon it crouched low and began to edge toward Raan. Massive paws padded the ground like the earth was liquid, allowing the catlike creature to float over its surface. The creature's serpentine tail twitched and curled in the air as if it were charged by unseen electricity.

Again, Raan called in the nonsense voice as loud as a trumpet, and the Chimera stopped, looking intent on its prey. They were now close enough to feel each other's heat. He didn't know how long his bluff would last.

[24]
Battle on the Brink

HE STOOD EYE TO EYE with the beast. The scent of fur and sweat overwhelmed him. Panting puffs of vapor came from both their nostrils. He felt the sticky blood of his blistered hand as he gripped his hatchet. The tree spanned the chasm, but it was too late to cross. Both man and monster stared each other down, frozen, alert, Chimera ready to pounce, Raan poised to spring to his hopeless defense and his one chance to drive his axe between the eyes of the enormous face. Then a crazy idea came to him.

As the creature crouched to strike, Raan drew the stone from around his neck and dangled it in front of the animal, swinging it like a pendulum. Back and forth, back and forth, the yellow eyes followed the white stone from side to side. Seconds became minutes, and the huge eyes began to glaze over, hypnotized. Time froze, and Raan could feel his pulse throbbing. Carefully, slowly, not daring a sudden move, he retreated, while dangling the slowly swinging stone as the Chimera stared.

He was halfway across his makeshift bridge when the beast awoke from its trance. With a ravenous snarl and bound, it was on the bridge, claws out. Suddenly, the slender span crumpled, sending Raan and the Chimera careening into the rapids below.

Raan was lucky to land in a channel of the gushing torrent, but the creature's body hit hard on the rocks and was gone in a rush of foam. Raan swept along in the whitewater, shooting the rapids, bobbing on the current, swirling, dunking, and popping up for air. Buffeted by huge boulders, he gasped breaths between underwater somersaults. Somehow, he kept his head and managed to position his feet downstream to avoid collisions with the larger rocks.

When the water calmed, and he dog paddled to shore covered by bruises and blood. Raan's throbbing body fell forward, his hands sinking into the ooze of the riverbank, but he managed to crawl. A deep fog came off the river, swallowing him in a world of dreamlike gray. Glop, glob, slop, flop, flop, glop, he slid himself through the muck to drier ground. Exhausted, he froze on hands and knees cemented to the ground like a statue, powerless and directionless, too spent to think.

As if in a dream, he noticed a pair of old shoes and two legs standing before him; if they had a body, it was veiled by the fog. He rubbed his eyes and tried to clear his drowsiness. The nightmare remained, and the shoes slowly stepped away. Raan followed on all fours, crawling like an exhausted beast. He lost track of his aching knees and intently focused on the old brown shoes leading him like a silent piper. Finally, he placed his hand on a set of stone steps. A wisp of wind blew away the fog, and before him, he saw a stone archway and a heavy wooden door.

"The castle," Raan whispered. The ghostly shoes were gone.

He rose to his knees and pounded on the door with his remaining strength. Just as he began to lose consciousness, the door opened, and there, backlit in yellow light, stood Koal.

I stumble through life as a clumsy amateur, knowing nothing good comes without the Divine touch. So, I wait for those moments when I sense His nearness. Teach me, O King, to wait with joy and cheerful expectation, knowing that patient faith will be rewarded.
(From the Journals of Zambo the Mute)

[25] TRAPPED

GENTLE RAIN FILTERED THROUGH a green canopy as unseen breezes sent showers of cascading droplets to serenade the quiet wood in a concert of tree music. Two squirrels played tag, leaping between limbs of a nearby tree, chattering with calls and conversation not meant for people's ears. A gray-brown rabbit moved furtively through the wet grass, twitching whiskers, suddenly springing away when a pair of sparrows landed nearby. The birds pecked a couple of pecks, looked at him, and then leaped into the air. From his favorite bench in Central Park, he looked out from his umbrella and breathed the scents of nutmeg and cloves mingled with lilac and fresh-cut grass. Dewy greenery glowed in the coming light, riding the wings of the Hudson River wind.

The pleasant dream faded, and Raan rose from the cotton-ball comfort of sleep to feel hard, cold stones against his cheek. Opening one eye, he saw an out-of-focus arm with a torn shirt sleeve smudged with reddish-brown bloodstains. He opened the other, and a flood of wakefulness flowed in. Quickly closing both eyes, he yearned to return to the dream, but there was no escape back into bliss.

He remembered the Chimera, his fall, and the rapids. He painfully recalled the castle door and the image of Koal gloating over him. His ribs and back screamed in pain. Reaching to scratch an itch behind his ear, he felt a patch of dried blood. How long have I been unconscious? he wondered.

Trying to stand, he felt the room spin furiously and fell over. He tried again, lost balance, and fell, bumping his head on the pavers. Dauntless, he experimented with different body positions and was finally able to gain his knees by cocking his head to one side and slowly rising at an angle. Balance, he thought, is grossly underrated.

Once upright, he patted himself down and checked for injuries, assessing the tender spots, but he found no broken bones. His pockets were empty, so he was without a knife, compass, money, or shoes. Surprisingly, he found the white stone still on its string around his neck, and when he touched it, he heard the words in the back of his mind: "Be patient; everything will turn out okay." He sighed a long, slow sigh; he had no choice but to go on and believe the ghostly promise.

Raan saw that he was in a round room with stone walls and a thick wooden door. A shaft of light came from an arched window high above, illuminating countless specks of floating dust. Shadows hid the ceiling. He noticed heavy iron rings hanging from spikes driven into the walls. Chains dangled from the rings, and he pulled himself up by a chain and held on to a ring to keep steady as he stood.

"This place must be inside a tower or turret of the castle," he said aloud to break the silence. Steadying himself with his hands, he moved along the wall and nudged the door. It was locked. The stones of the walls were old, and the mortar had fallen out in places, leaving sizable gaps. Moisture had seeped through a few cracks and puddled in several low spots. As he stood quietly trying to think, he heard a scratching noise, and to his surprise, a mouse popped out of one of the openings, scrambled nimbly across the floor, and mounted the wall using the larger cracks as a stairway. In a few minutes, it disappeared into the dark recesses of the ceiling.

"I wonder where the little guy went?" Raan thought aloud and walked to get a closer view of the wall. Suddenly, a loud clacking, clunk, and moaning of door hinges caused him to turn. He was shocked; in the doorway stood Koal with a drawn sword in one hand and a plate of food in the other. Neither spoke, but the two locked eyes, and it seemed as if a line of fire bridged their faces.

Koal pointed the weapon at Raan's chest. Raan didn't move. Slowly, Koal lowered the plate to the ground and silently slipped out.

Raan sprang to the door, shouting, "Koal, wait! What's going on? Let's talk about this! Koal, wait!"

There was no reply except receding footsteps. Raan was alone. He thought about the two men in the music emporium, his Midtown flat, his cats, the dog he wanted to have, and the homeless street people he'd give change to every day and wondered how he would get out of this mess. Yet somehow he knew he would. He ravenously devoured the plate of gruel, two mushrooms, and a crust of dry bread.

[26] Secret Ways

SHORTLY AFTER EATING, RAAN began to feel strange. First, the room started to sway from side to side, and then the walls and floor appeared to bend in unnatural directions. Inside his mind came visions of gigantic mice, purple dragons, and upside-down sailboats in the clouds. He felt like he was floating backward in a river of chocolate syrup. The unstoppable dream swirled around him until he vomited into the waste-hole, and all went dark.

Raan awoke from the hallucination, soaked in cold sweat.

"What just happened to me?" he said.

Just saying the words aloud helped him refocus. Using the walls to steady him, he hobbled around the chamber and uttered every verse of poetry,

Scripture, or speech he could remember. He sang snippets of pop songs and ballads he'd written, choruses from show tunes, and old campfire songs. They must have sounded like nonsense, but it helped clear his mind. He even prayed the most earnest prayers he could think of, not believing anyone could hear him, but slowly, his mind became steady.

He called to Koal until his voice was hoarse, and hearing no reply, he collapsed into a heap by the wall across from the door. Unexpectedly, the door opened, and another plate was slid into the room. The door slammed shut, and Raan heard a chuckle.

"Koal! Koal!" The silence was complete. Raan stared hungrily at the food but was too tired to eat.

In a little while, he heard a scratching sound again and noticed another mouse shyly sniffing its way toward the plate. As Raan looked on, the creature nibbled at a mushroom, and in a few seconds, the critter's whiskers and tail began to twitch strangely. The rodent started to squeak and hop about convulsively, turning in many circles until it lay motionless. Raan watched helplessly and then crawled to the mouse and picked it up. Holding it gently in his cupped hands, he breathed on it warmly.

Strangely, Raan found himself praying for the little rodent, his only companion in the forsaken place. Praying wasn't his thing, and he didn't expect anything to happen, but a lot of really odd things had happened during his adventure. After a while, its chest began to move as the tiny mouse slept in Raan's hands.

Raan carefully held the little fellow as it dozed until it slowly began breathing normally. It seemed so precious, yet so vulnerable. Raan's suspicions rose, as did his anger. Was it poisoned? he wondered looking at the plate of food, and then he remembered reading about certain kinds of mushrooms that caused hallucinations. Just then, the mouse came to life, looked at him in terror, and bounded out of Raan's hands, skittering across the room.

The mouse began to climb the wall just below the window. It climbed a few feet, returned to the floor, looked straight at Raan, twitched its whiskers, and flicked its tail once to the left and twice to the right. Then it climbed again two feet, turned around, and repeated the same gestures.

"Are you trying to tell me something, little fellow?" Raan asked gently.

The mouse turned and repeated the entire performance one last time before it scampered up the wall in a free solo that would make any mountaineer proud, disappearing over the ledge at the top.

Raan reached for the stone dangling on its thong under his shirt. In a still, quiet voice, Raan heard the word "Follow."

"That's impossible," blurted Raan.

"You're so sure about what you can't do. Follow," said the voice irresistibly.

So Raan followed the mouse by wedging his fingers into the larger cracks and twisting them to hold his weight. He climbed, sticking his toes wherever he could feel a ledge, pulling with gnarled fingers and pushing with shoeless feet. Finally, surprised and exhausted, he wrapped both arms on the ledge and struggled over. As he caught his breath, he saw before him a trap door eaten away with age that opened into what looked like a well of black ink. The top of a ladder stuck out from the opening.

Resting atop the ledge, he surveyed his prison. He saw the carved timbers of a sloping roof and the dust-covered window. Curved walls met at pillars on opposite sides and a wedge of light came in from the gap below the door. Sunbeams from the window cast the rough image of a cross on the mottled floor.

On the ledge, he was surprised to notice a coil of rope, a spool of string, and an empty bottle. Raan wondered what to do next. He was famished but didn't trust the food dish now he'd seen what had happened to the mouse. He debated with himself:

"Are you going to climb the ladder and see where it leads?"

"Maybe, but what if it's a trap?"

"You are already in a trap? What if it's a way out?"

"But what if Koal comes back and finds me missing? He'd figure out where I've gone and kill me for sure."

"It seems like he is already trying to kill you. Or worse, make you crazy by poisoning your mind."

"Maybe someone will come looking for me."

"Koal will say you never arrived."

As Raan continued to ponder his options, he heard sounds outside the door! He didn't want to be discovered yet, so he quickly tied one end of the rope to the top of the ladder and, trusting his luck, scrabbled back to the prison floor in the nick of time. Pushing the rope into the shadows, he threw himself into a heap on the wall opposite the door just as it opened.

A man in the doorway stood silhouetted in the light behind him. It wasn't Koal. He held a sword in a drooping right hand and another bowl of food in the other. He was trembling and spoke in stammers,

"The master Koal bids me check on you and bring you more food. Are you well?"

Raan didn't know what to say or do. He was still exhausted from the river, the poisoned food, and the climb, so he realized he couldn't overpower this armed man in his present state. He decided to fake it and spoke slowly in halting words,

"Where ... is Koal? Why ... am I ... here?" gesturing to his surroundings.

"Where else should we put a thief?" said the man.

"But I'm ... not a thief. I ... came to visit ... the prince by ... his invitation."

"I was told you'd say something like that." The man set the bowl on the floor, stepped back, and slammed the door behind him.

Raan's blood boiled.

"It's true! I'm here at the request of the prince!" Raan shouted. But his words were lost on the heavy oak door.

His anger gave him strength, and he used the rope to climb back to the ledge, trying to calm himself and decide on his next step. Carefully, he tested the ladder's top rung; it was solid. Then he tested the next one, and soon he was at the bottom in total darkness. It was like being at the bottom of a well looking up; the dim light at the top of the opening seemed a blaze. He tied an end of the string he found to the bottom of the ladder. A little insurance to guide me back, thought the blind man as he turned to face the blackness. The bright opening above seemed like safety, but Raan knew it was only a window back to prison.

He crept along the passage in silence, using his senses of smell and hearing as much as his hands. Strangely, he felt more alert than ever and unusually invigorated. At last, after moving slowly for what seemed like an eternity, he saw a pencil-thin sliver of light ahead. It seemed to be floating in space. One end of the golden beam faded into darkness, and the other ended at a keyhole.

Noiselessly, he traced the frame of a small door and found a latch. Listening, he thought he heard the faint sound of snoring in the room beyond. Gingerly, he tried the latch and heard a click, then held his breath. The rhythm of the sleeper beyond changed a beat but then resumed as before. Carefully, he cracked the door open until he saw a large ornate four-poster bed piled with lavish bedclothes, and half under them lay a twisted old man twitching and turning as if dreaming frightful dreams. This might be the prince, but why is he asleep in the middle of the day? Raan urgently wanted to speak with the sleeper but another time—now, he began to worry that Koal or his guard might return any moment, so he retraced his path to his prison cell and contemplated his three days in captivity—and as the light disappeared from the lone window, he began to feel a little hope.

[27]
A Conspiracy of Two

CASY BEGAN TO FEEL UNEASY after Raan had been gone for three days. She confided in GB.

"I don't know if I'm imagining things, but I'm worried about Raan. Call it intuition or whatever you want; something doesn't feel right. There are too many unknowns, and what if something happens to him on the way, or something's wrong at the castle?

"I've been thinking the same thing, Casy. That's a long way to go alone, even for Raan. What do you think we should do?"

"There's only one thing we can do; we must follow him."

"Seth will never let you go. You know you're . . . and . . ." GB caught himself mid-sentence, trying to be sensitive, but the meaning of his verbal stumble shouted loud and clear.

"You think just because I'm a woman and, well, I have this crutch, that I can't go. Well, you're mistaken, GB. I can do anything I put my mind to. Besides, I got you!" She lightly laughed; her bright, confident face was like a shower of apple blossoms.

GB blushed and took a little bow as he considered the options.

"But how do we get Seth on board? He'd be a big help, yet I doubt he'd let you travel so far."

"We may have to forget to mention it to him," said Casy, balancing on one foot as she took down a jar of flour from the upper shelf and started making bread for dinner.

[28] SHOCKING TRUTH

OVER THE NEXT FEW DAYS, Raan explored many corridors, doors, stairways, and ladders in the dark labyrinth, uncoiling the thread on his way out and recoiling to find his way back while making a mental map of the maze. He'd pour the poisoned food down the waste hole and make sure he loudly shouted deliriously and sang nonsense songs when he wasn't exploring. He found unseen lookout spots in all the rooms and halls and confirmed the location of Koal's private chamber and that the fitful man he'd encountered on his first venture was indeed Prince Terrion.

One of his first discoveries was a hidden ledge that overlooked the kitchen. Once, while helping himself to a few scraps of food, he heard footsteps, so he nimbly regained his hiding place and learned a terrible secret.

Invisibly perched above, Raan saw Koal enter carrying a serving tray and watched as the sinister figure busied himself making a bowl of porridge, whistling and humming as if preparing a casserole for a church potluck. Koal pulled down a covered jar, and with gloved hands and a pair of tongs, he carefully removed several mushrooms from the vessel. Mincing them with precision, he stirred the pieces into the bubbling gruel.

"This little gift will keep my lord the prince in bed and babbling for another day," chuckled Koal under his breath. Sneering at the bowl of porridge, he fixed an unhappy expression on his face and called for one of the kitchen staff. "Server!" When the young man entered, Koal carelessly placed the tray in his hands, causing the serving lad to fumble a touch. "Watch what you're doing!" Koal growled. "If you spill the prince's breakfast, how will he ever regain his strength?"

Raan was so shocked that he almost gasped aloud. Now he knew why the prince was trapped in bed and couldn't move—the mushrooms were drugging him. Koal led the server out of the kitchen, so Raan scrambled to the prince's bedroom just in time to spy Koal hand-feeding the poisoned gruel to the prince with fake compassionate care. The prince did his best to sit up while eating, smiling at the feigned kindness, but gratefully fell back into his bed, weaker than before.

Raan was livid, but what could he do, barely alive himself? Koal would kill him, saying he was a thief or plotting against Terrion. Faced with this helpless gambit, Raan retreated into the darkness, following the thread of hope back to the light of his dungeon to figure out what to do. He had to tell someone, but he didn't know who he could trust. He didn't want to reveal his ability to move about unseen until he knew he was certain to rescue the prince. One thing was sure: he had to stop Koal from poisoning Terrion. But how?

[29] The Perfect Conversation Partner

KOAL HAD THE HABIT of talking to his dog, Conga. In its prime, the giant wolfhound was a fierce hunter, but age had left it quite docile except for its bark. It spent most of its days lying by the fire, growling at mice or sniffing for morsels under the dining table. For Koal, Conga was a perfect conversation partner, always available and never contradictory.

"Why did Raan come, and who else knew?" said Koal under his breath as he plopped himself into a comfortable chair. A long-fingered hand reached down to scratch Conga behind the ears, and the big dog's tail pounded the floor in delight.

"Do you think they know about the plan, Ole boy? Dad is too deeply into it to say anything, but one of his cronies might for the right price. I can't trust anyone except you." He reached over to the table and cut off a piece of cheese and gave it to Conga, who snarfed it up in one gulp.

"But what should we do about Raan?" Koal continued talking to the dog, who closed its eyes. Then he mused quietly, "No one should ever know he arrived." What do you think? Should we keep Raan as our caged guest forever?" He fiendishly grinned, "I'll say the beast must have gotten him. They'll believe anything. Anyway, soon he won't even know his name."

Koal poured himself a drink from a silver-studded leather flask and sat back, contemplating their plan, which he narrated to the sleeping dog:

"Once we win the old prince's heart, I'll become his ward. So far, things have been going well. Once the prince trusts me completely, I'll stop the poison and provide a fake remedy, and make it appear as though I've cured the prince. In gratitude, the prince will have the perfect reason to make me his ward and heir. When the time comes, the prince will fall ill again and die, leaving everything to us." The wolfhound twitched in his dreams and said nothing about the elaborate scheme.

Koal's eyes began to feel heavy, so he placed his cup on the table and contemplated what he would do with the treasure and fell asleep in his chair.

If Koal had been more alert, he might have noticed a flicker of movement in the rafters as Raan nimbly climbed back into the secret passage.

[30]
ALMOST A MIRACLE

THE TWO CONSPIRATORS eased the cart along the back road from the feedstore, avoiding small talk because there was much to think about. It had been five days since Raan's departure, and they still hadn't heard anything—tomorrow they'd follow him! The sky was crystal clear, and the two travelers enjoyed the beauty of the mulberry orchards in full bloom with yellow-green clusters and noticed countless white dots amid the branches where silkworms wove their cocoons.

"To think that all the wealth of our land begins with a worm learning to fly," said GB, hoping to interest Casy with a deep thought. But Casy wanted to stay focused so they could finish getting ready for the trip and keep it secret.

"There you go again, Professor Boing!" Casy said, hoping GB could be kept from launching into a full dissertation before lunch. "I can't keep up with your brain."

"Sorry, I get carried away sometimes, but the change is almost a miracle."

"It is a miracle! One of the little everyday miracles that happen all around us," said Casy, taking her turn at philosophy.

GB looked curious and asked, "What miracles?"

"I'm talking about how an eagle soars through the sky, how an oak tree grips the earth, how a mighty king learns to walk. They're all miracles in a way."

"Now you're playing the philosopher and poet!" said GB, smiling.

"Well, I guess so, sort of. If we have time, I'll tell you a story that Seth heard from the old hermit on the other side of the mountain," said Casy, keeping pace with the limber Bibgit, who had just hopped out of the cart and was busy unloading. Casy kept track of the goods on her ledger and ensured everything was organized; the supplies they needed for the trip were hidden in the cart, while GB quickly moved everything else to the barn.

When they finished, the two sat in the shade of a large pear tree. The fruit was on the way to being ripe but wasn't quite ready. A feathery breeze blew in from the mountains, and children played nearby, trying to catch butterflies on a lawn. The shady tree was inviting, and the two conspirators enjoyed the break from their work.

Casy said, "I think we have time, so I can tell you the story if you'd like. It won't take long."

"I guess I've been playing the professor a lot; I think it's time for me to do some listening. I remember hearing an old graybeard in the colony tell me, 'A man can't learn anything with his mouth open.'"

They both laughed and settled down in the grass letting the light filtering through the pear tree bathe them in a surrealistic glow. To GB, Casy's voice sounded magical. She rarely told stories, but whenever she said something, it was usually profound. GB focused on his friend, and Casy began.

[31] To Catch the Wind

THERE WAS ONCE A SUCCESSFUL young man who prospered in everything he did and became very wealthy. He enjoyed his life to the fullest but felt something was missing in his heart. So he investigated politics and philosophy, but they left him feeling conflicted. So, he began to travel the world and experience its cultures, music, art, and natural beauty, but in time, his emptiness returned. Then, he began to study religions of every type, reading many books and listening to so many wise teachers that he couldn't keep track of them all, but alas, after years, he still felt empty inside.

One day, he heard about a prophet who lived on the side of a volcano on a remote island and was said to possess the wisdom of the King of the gods. He thought that the prophet might have the key to what was missing in his heart.

The man spent his fortune to reach the island and endured shipwrecks, storms, and many adventures until he clambered through the jungle, across a desert, and finally up the steep side of the volcano, which fortunately was not erupting at the time. Scratched and bruised, with clothes in rags, he came exhausted to the hut where the prophet lived.

He knocked at the rickety door, but no one was there, and just as he was about to collapse in despair, he saw the thinnest, most wrinkly, jolliest little man skipping toward him.

"So here you are at last," said a voice that sounded like bubbles in the sunshine. "I've been watching you for weeks and waiting for you today, trying to catch the wind."

"Have you caught it?" asked the man, a bit skeptical of the strange man, wondering if his quest was a good idea.

"Of course not; you can't catch the wind, but you can have a jolly bit of fun trying. Impossible challenges keep me humble, and I can use all the practice I can get." The prophet did a pirouette that made it seem like he was walking on air. "Welcome! You must be tired and hungry too. Come in, welcome to my humble abode."

The old prophet's smile was so big and his bow so gracious that the man immediately began to feel at ease. The prophet fed him fruit he had never tasted, which was magical because, after a few bites, the eater felt completely satisfied. There was also a delicious soup that the prophet said came from roots grown in volcanic soil. There was milk from goats of the volcano that, after a few sips, sent a tingling sensation through his entire body, and he felt as if his hair had grown a few inches in less than a minute.

The prophet told stories and sang songs, and the two laughed a lot, but alas, the time came for the younger man to ask the question he'd come to ask:

"Why do I feel empty inside?"

The look of compassion on the older man's face was soft and thoughtful and had a glimmer of hope, but the visitor slumped despondently. The bright-eyed prophet tenderly took the man's hands, lifted him upright, and said, "Sit up, friend. That's nothing to be down about; it's easy to fix!"

"What must I learn?" asked the man, "I've already studied long and sat at the feet of venerable sages, yet I still feel the emptiness."

"Take hope, my son. You've learned so much; maybe it's time for you to unlearn some things," said the prophet with an understanding nod.

"That sounds confusing. Please teach me what you mean?" The man mentally prepared himself to be led down another vague, paradoxical road like others with clever words had taught him in the past.

"Some things cannot be taught; this I must show, and you must do," said the prophet, leading the man to a large, flat rock shaped like a table.

The sun was brilliant. He produced a dazzling crystal glass from an oak chest and filled it with clear water. It radiated the sunlight in a thousand directions. Next, he produced another crystal glass, set it next to the first, and filled it with muddy water. It was so dark that the water cast a shadow. The two crystal glasses stood in the same sunlight; one sparkled, and the other only made shadows.

"I see it!" said the man. "The muddy water doesn't let the light through, and the muddy glass is me!" He looked down, perplexed. "But how do I refill my glass?"

"Often unlearning takes longer than learning," said the prophet, "and is more difficult. Are you willing to unlearn?"

"Yes," the man said without hesitation, "I want to be clear inside so I can be filled with light. That's what's missing in my heart!"

So the prophet took the man to a small fishing village and showed him how to clean fish. And so he cleaned fish to help an old fisherman whose hands were too stiff to hold a knife. He learned to sail, mend the nets, and find where the fish were. He smelled like fish, thought about fish, tasted fish in everything, and dreamed of fish, but in time, despite the relentless work, he learned to love the aged fisherman, who, even though he was infirm and in pain, taught him by example to labor faithfully with all his ability.

After a time, the prophet returned and took the man to a shop and gave him a set of tools. People began to bring him broken items to fix. He did his best to repair everything, but some items were abused, and others were too old and beyond repair. So people scorned him and even accused him of making things worse. As hard as he worked to help the people, he couldn't please them all, and some became bitter. He started loathing life and couldn't stand going to work or seeing another person enter his shop. One afternoon, a little girl arrived in tears, holding the cutest doll he'd ever seen. He didn't know which was prettier, the girl or the doll. With one arm, she cradled her baby doll, and in the other hand, she held its arm, somehow broken at the shoulder.

"Oh, dear! Who do you have here?" he said in the gentlest voice he could while looking into the girl's sobbing face with genuine compassion.

The girl sniffed, took a breath, and sobbed, trying to hold back the tears, "My baby's hurt, and I don't know what to do."

"Let me have a look at her," he said, kneeling to her level and reaching out to take the doll and severed arm as tenderly as if he were handling the king's jewels.

"Will she be okay?"

"I think so. What happened to her?"

"Bojo, my brother's dog, tried to eat her."

"Oh my, what a mean dog."

"Oh no, Bojo is a good dog; he doesn't know any better. He thought she was a toy. He's only a dog, and that's what dogs do," she said in a sad but understanding tone.

The girl's wise words and forgiveness for the reckless dog took him aback.

"Let me see what I can do for her," he said as he quickly mended the arm and returned the doll to the girl as good as new. Once the girl was gone, he thought about his situation and began to think about the complaining customers in a different light. He remembered the girl's words and thought, They didn't know any better, so he started seeing his customers empathetically, feeling in some small way his listening ear might fix more than his nimble hands.

Eventually, the prophet returned and took the man to a large restaurant, gave him a guitar, and told him to sing songs to the guests. Each night, the man sang all the songs he knew. But every night, the guests asked him to sing songs they liked better but he didn't know, and when he tried to sing them, they laughed at him, made rude faces, and said other restaurants had better singers.

Night after night for many weeks, he sang and endured the patrons' disdain, and the man became very low, then bitter, then angry, then cold, but he continued to act cheerful until one night, he thought he couldn't sing any longer and planned to give up.

Walking home, he noticed a man and a woman sitting on a bench crying. They said they'd just lost their only child in an accident. Not knowing what else he could do, the man took his guitar and sang a sad song to the couple. When he finished, they asked him to sing another, then another. As he poured out his heart in sad love songs to the grieving parents, he began to see a change in them. Soon, the two looked at each other, clasped hands, and said, "We can do this." With a nod of thanks, they left the man, who continued to play his songs of sadness into the night.

The next day at the restaurant, the man looked at the customers differently; he saw each of them as a person with a hidden story. He thought behind each face was a universe of experience and motivations, and each came to the restaurant with deep needs. As he sang that evening, he sang to those needs, hoping one of the songs might help someone somehow.

And by and by, one night, as he looked at the full moon passing among the clouds, he realized he no longer felt he was missing something. The next day, he trudged his way back up the volcano only to find that the old prophet had died in his sleep the night before.

Solemnly, he buried the saint and placed a cross he had carved himself in the volcanic ground by the old prophet's head as a marker. Gravely, he returned to the hut and reverently looked around. He found the prophet's books, his cooking gear, his clothes, and his tools. Most importantly, he found the prophet's journal and began glancing through it. On the last page was a note, scribbled in haste: Now your story begins. Live it well!

From then on, the man took his place in the hut on the side of the volcano and lived there in peace to the end of his days.

GB looked up after Casy finished feeling like hours had passed even though it only took a few minutes. He wondered what to make of this young woman who was both beautiful and wise. He decided he wouldn't try to understand her and let her words soak into his soul. He said, "Thanks Casy, that was a great story! I'd love to learn it."

"You're welcome my friend, I'm glad you liked it. Maybe we can get Seth to tell it sometime. He tells it so much better than I do. In the meantime we'd better get moving. Are you ready?"

"I'm ready for anything. Let's go!"

[32] Catapulted Into Disaster

As he explored the hidden passages, Raan had learned to pad quietly in the dark, feeling, hearing, sensing the subtle changes in the air, tasting it as much as smelling and feeling it on his skin.

He learned to walk without stubbing his toes and knew whether he was going up or down by subtle changes in the ground beneath his feet. Having the stone gave him confidence, and the blackness became a comfort.

He remembered a verse from the days his parents took him to Sunday school:

> Surely the darkness shall cover me,
>
> and the light about me be night,
>
> Even the darkness is not dark to you;
>
> The night is as bright as the day,
>
> For darkness is as light with you.

One strange thing he couldn't understand was that he thought he sometimes heard footsteps in the corridors. They were like light bare feet furtively padding as if to escape being discovered. He was sure they weren't an echo, but he couldn't be certain he wasn't imagining them. One thing was sure: if they were real, whoever it was seemed more afraid of him than he was of them.

On the morning of his fourth day in prison, his adventure nearly ended when, while exploring a deep passage, he slipped, slid down a steep tunnel, was launched into space, and plunged into an underground pool. The icy water gripped him like an iron fist and stole his breath. He couldn't swim, so he gasped for air while kicking his feet and trying to find the bottom. With flailing arms struggling to keep his head above the surface, Raan quickly became exhausted, so in a desperate act of faith, he prayed a one-word prayer, "Help!" and wished with all his heart that God was real.

Instantly, calm flooded Raan's mind, and hidden instincts took over. He relaxed, grabbed a breath, and went under. Sweeping up with his arms palms upward, his body sank until his feet struck the bottom. His chest felt as if it would burst, but he stayed calm and pushed off with all his force. In a few long seconds, his head popped out, and he grabbed another breath and went down again.

When he hit bottom, he could feel that the stony lake bed was sloped, so he pushed off toward shallower water. Bobbing to the surface, he seized another mouthful of air and went under. Over and over, he grabbed a new breath and went down again. Each time, he repeated the pattern, pushing off toward the shallows until, finally, his hands brushed against the pool's rocky edge, and he managed to drag his body over the slippery stones until he reached a dry shelf and collapsed.

Panting gratefully, he gulped for breath after breath. His pulse hammered in his temples, so he forced himself to breathe slowly and deeply until he regained control. But then he reached for the stone and found it was gone! He felt everywhere around him, scrambling all the way to the water's edge and found nothing. Somewhere in the dark within dark at the bottom of the pool was the friend he'd counted on being there whenever he needed.

The ebony world swallowed him, while rage overcame his heart. At the top of his voice, he cried into the void, "Voice, who are you? What are you? Why am I even in this forsaken place? I'm done! I'll sit and die here alone, undiscovered. I didn't even ask for this crazy adventure!"

Raan planted his rump on a stone, propping his elbows on his knees and covering his ears with his hands. He pouted stubbornly until he finally broke down and wept.

"I don't call this place forsaken," said a gentle voice so close that Raan was startled out of his gloom.

"Who's there!" yelled Raan, thrashing his arms violently in every direction at once.

"I am here," said the voice as if whispering in Raan's left ear.

Spinning around to try to touch the source of the voice, Raan lost his balance, stumbled, hit his head, and passed out.

He dreamed he was standing alone atop a tall mountain spire—a needle in the air where every side dropped a thousand feet or more in a sheer cliff. To the north, he saw a vast mountain range whose gray-blue and white peaks trailed off into the distance. To the west, his eyes beheld a sprawling desert stretching across the horizon etched with deep shadows and brown and gold curves. To the south, an expanse of fertile fields and lush valleys reached the edge of sight, giving off a greenish glow in the setting sun.

There were no stairs, no path of any kind. It was like standing on an island in the sky. Suddenly he felt a cool breeze caressing his back and neck. He turned around and faced east, startled by the sight of a glorious mountain shimmering in the sunset. It towered high above his vantage point, its peak out of sight, with sides covered in deep greens, grays, browns, and a forest of many kinds of trees. He saw cascading waterfalls playfully dancing on their way to the lowlands and stripes of snow through parting clouds. He felt a low throbbing sound, deeper than he could hear—a gentle but unstoppable power surrounding and engulfing him in waves of what he could only describe as wholesomeness—humble but immensely strong. The tower he stood upon seemed like a sandcastle in comparison. Without thinking—he didn't know why—he knelt.

Then he saw a rope and plank bridge spanning the chasm between his stone spire and the opposite ridge. It was thin and so long that the far side of it seemed only a thread against the backdrop of the mountainside. A few gentle mists like gossamer threads floated in the canyon, giving the span a ghostlike aura. Fear gripped him. He knew his only escape from the spire was to trust this narrow way. Trust, he thought, is such an unusual word. I take it for granted. But what do I trust—really trust? Nothing much, he confessed.

He shuddered as he watched the bridge sway in the wind. He wished he were brave enough, but he couldn't believe something that thin and unstable could hold him as he was out in the gulf alone, exposed, with thousands of feet of air below him and the entire limits of the sky above. Yet he knew the only choices were to stay atop this island prison until he died of thirst, exposure, and despair, or escape across the slender span to the mountain.

While this internal debate raged, he noticed a speck of white moving over the bridge. He watched as the speck became a person running quickly and effortlessly toward him. Soon he realized the person was an older woman, so old that Raan marveled at how she could move so gracefully and quickly across the slender bridge. When she neared Raan, he recognized her as the old woman he had met near the start of his adventure before the featherlight race, Emma. Her smile was as radiant as ever, but her body was as young as an athletic tween's. She called him and said, "Come, follow me; everything will be okay!" She turned and bounded back across.

He was left gaping. Astonished, he walked to the bridge. He stared at the expanse, touched the backstays and tower poles, and studied the floor beams and ropes, but couldn't make himself take the first step. It was not that he didn't trust the bridge; he didn't trust himself to make it all the way.

He woke to the starless night of the cave. "Am I still dreaming?" he said aloud. He felt the words in the air more real than the thoughts in his mind. Reaching out, he felt the rocks, pressing into them with the palms of his hands, passing his fingers over the rough surface. He sensed their wetness and scratched them with his nails; he heard the scratching. "You're real enough," said Raan as he checked his body and moved. The wet clothes stuck to his clammy skin; as uncomfortable as it felt, they were real. Running his fingers through his hair, he yelped as a jab of sharp pain stabbed him when he touched the spot where his head had hit the rock. He felt fresh blood and, bringing his bloodied hand to his mouth, tasted its sweet saltiness. It was real. Somehow, the pain, the hardness, and the simple realities of taste and touch convinced him.

"I'm awake," he said. "I defy you, blackness. Do your worst; you will not daunt my soul!"

Of course, Raan was bluffing, but even his bluff showed that he still had a spark of courage. His entire universe was just the cave, the ground, the scents, the cool air on his lips as he breathed in, and the warm air passing them when he breathed out. The resonant echoes of droplets and running water and the rustlings of his movements stirred his curiosity. He heard his voice echoing all around him as he yelled, "I am, I'm here, I'm alive!" Over and over he called out until he was sure his focus had returned. But when the echoes died away, the actual weight of his situation fully fell on him—he was alone—completely and utterly alone, with no friends, no way, no stone, and no hope.

Then, fully facing the darkest spark of his inner self, he knelt and said, "I need you Voice, or God, whatever you are, whoever you are. I know You are real, but I've been fighting You all along. I'm tired of fighting. You win. Do with me what You will! Even if You leave me here to die, I am yours."

At that moment deep in the earth, Raan experienced a feeling he'd never encountered. The word he used to describe it later was smooth. Before, his life was edgy and rough, but now he felt smooth and clear. He then had a vision of something he couldn't explain. But he knew the vision was real. It was like he had stepped onto the rope bridge of his dream and discovered he had an unquenchable desire to run across. His fear was gone!

Thinking of the voice that had spoken to him earlier, Raan asked again: "Are you still there? Or were you part of the dream?"

"Some might call me a dream come true, but others might think of me as their worst nightmare," said the voice, as close as before.

Raan waved his hands about his head as if he was swatting an invisible insect, but nothing was there. Yet he had no fear.

"Well, for me," he said, "being trapped in this dark cavern, all wet, bloody, alone, and lost, is my worst nightmare. At least 'you're someone I can talk to."

There was a long silencc, and Raan bcgan to miss the ghostly voice.

"Can I talk to you, voice? Will you talk to me? I'm terrified, and I want to trust you. Will you be-tray my trust?"

"Trust is not easily given, so I'm honored by yours. Even if I could betray your trust, I wouldn't. Be refreshed." As the voice spoke, a wave of tingling swept through Raan; it started at his fingertips and spread throughout his body, from his toenails to the edges of his ears. Afterward, he felt restored. And not just in his spirit. He was perfectly dry, his head no longer hurt, the blood and gash on his scalp had disappeared, even the scrapes on his knees and hands were gone, and he was no longer hungry.

Stunned but bursting with delight, Raan stood up and almost danced. "Who are you? What are you?"

"I'm me, only me. I was, and I am, and will be."

"But that's not a proper name," Raan said. Where do you come from? Do you live in this cave?"

"I come from nowhere and am everywhere. And Raan, I see you."

Raan was startled, "How do you know my name, and how can you see me? It's completely dark."

"Even the darkness is like light to me," said the voice.

Raan thought it strange that the voice just said the thing he'd thought about earlier, but said, "Voice, thank you for talking to me. Can you show me the way out?"

"There are many ways, but I can help you find the best way."

"Can . . . uh, will you show me now? I'm willing to follow."

"I will do even more; I'll restore your hope."

Raan asked many questions, but the voice didn't speak again. Soon his courage returned. It felt like a spring inside his heart was bubbling up with living water, filling his mind and limbs. Hope flooded him, and with it, desire, passion, curiosity, and vigor flowed into his arms and legs.

Springing into action, he set out by feeling his way along the shore, keeping the sound of water on his right and feeling the dry ground's slope on his left. He sang. Nearby, he heard the gurgling of what must have been a small waterfall, and he could tell he was in a large cavern by the echoes of his voice. In the echoing sounds, he sensed when he was near a wall and where the open spaces were. In this way, he chose his course, wishing he could see it.

After his fall, he had lost all sense of direction, but navigating by sound, he thought he might find his passage again. Carefully, he navigated around the shore, feeling his way through the rocks toward the sound of flowing water. As strength returned to his limbs, hope rose within him, and he recognized that hope was a gift. He reached the waterfall and took a big drink, splashing cool water over his face and head. Revived, he crossed the stream and continued, the unchanging sound of the waterfall hissing in the impenetrable blackness, numbing him into a trancelike stupor, which he fought by counting his heartbeats. That was the only sense of time he had. He also counted the echoes of his voice. To stay alert, Raan began counting boulders as he crossed them.

Eventually, he began to smell something new. At first, he couldn't make out what it was, but after a while, he was sure it was the smell of wood, old and musty. The scent was unmistakable, like inside the old, dilapidated barn on his grandparents' Vermont farm.

Suddenly he was surprised when he put his hand on something wooden. It wasn't a tree root; it was a timber plank. He groped farther and found another, and then another, until he realized he had discovered some wooden machinery. He felt wheels and contraptions he couldn't understand without light. What was it doing deep underground? Maybe it was part of an abandoned mine. But his next find was even more amazing.

Near the wooden structure, his feet stepped in something gooey and cool between his toes—plain, ordinary mud, not rock. In a few feet the mud became dirt! After hours of stone tunnels, the dirt and little muddy puddles he stepped in were unmistakable and exciting! Immediately he abandoned the wooden structure and followed the dirt, which seemed to run parallel to the stream.

"A path!" said Raan, unable to contain himself.

Before long, gray light appeared, and soon he could discern the shadowy walls of the cave and glinting ripples in the stream flowing confidently forward. Full daylight was blinding, and Raan almost stepped off the edge of a cliff into a ravine. The stream became a waterfall as it fell carelessly in misty veils before it crashed upon the rocks below.

Raan steadied himself and collected his thoughts while he waited for his eyes to adjust. He was bursting with excitement but wary, keeping watch for other hazards. The castle was nowhere to be seen. Nowhere to be seen! He was outside the castle; he was free!

[33] DANGER WITHIN

IT WAS THE MORNING of the sixth day since Raan had left. Casy was up early, buzzing with excitement; today they were finally leaving. Seth was already gone, and she laid GB's breakfast on the table, but GB couldn't eat. She looked at her friend and studied his face. He was different this morning; usually, he was strong, somewhat cocky, almost defiant, but this morning, his head drooped, and his eyes looked down without their usual luster. This man was so different than her, but somehow, she suspected that in him, as in her, was some unspoken secret that cried out to be heard.

"Won't you eat something, my friend?" asked Casy as she placed a bowl of apple slices and candied walnuts on the table. "The cart is loaded and hitched; all it needs is us. I've packed the food."

GB remained motionless, lost in thought, rigid, and hardly breathing; he seemed not to notice Casy or the meal.

"Did you have trouble sleeping? I know it's exciting. I barely closed my eyes, but I'm eager to get going. Aren't you?" said Casy cheerfully, but when he didn't respond, she relaxed and changed her tone. "I can tell something's the matter, but I don't know how to help."

GB looked up a little, meeting Casy's gaze, and breathed slowly.

"Sometimes I feel like I'm losing my grip," said GB. "I feel miserable because of who I was and who I am, and I wonder if I have any future. I know I've been welcomed into the tribe, but that was only a ceremony on the mountain. Will they accept me in the day-to-day comings and goings of life? I wish I could be normal."

GB's unexpected confession surprised Casy; she wondered where the doubt came from, and then she thought, Maybe the third danger is doubt—a danger within. Kindly, she studied this man who had just opened up his soul to her. She wanted to say the right thing in the right way and respect his confidence. She prayed silently for wisdom.

"How can anyone know where they belong, GB? Some are guided by what seems like a heavenly escort into fruitful lives filled with a sense of purpose and understanding of their place. But we only see the outside of their lives. They have dark times, too, and feel the pinch of loss when it comes. Still, I imagine that title, creed, and pedigree help a little during the low times."

"I guess we all possess the same promise," replied GB, "but some lack honor. They show up at life's banquet without the right clothes and are turned away; I feel like a lonely cloud in a windless sky, hovering and waiting without much hope."

"Even a little hope is something," said Casy, "and a tiny spark of faith can change the world. What matters most is what you hope for and what you put your faith in." She thought a bit and said, "For you, the condition of your early life was tragic and outside of most people's experience. Because of your past, you're an awkward fit in some places. I feel the same." She gazed at her damaged foot. "Your childhood makes it hard for people to relate to you; perhaps they fear what they don't understand."

"What's that?" questioned GB.

"The raw belief and radical faith that you have," said Casy, "the faith that grows in toil and unpraised devotion. The faith you have is on the inside and more difficult to notice—"

"I don't want to be different," said GB. "I only want to belong to the Voice's family. I don't want position or influence; I only want to follow and be useful."

As he spoke, GB began to perk up. He ate some food and regained some of his usual spirit.

Casy smiled lovingly. "Your experiences also give you a humility that The Voice adores. Those without banquet clothes fail to realize that the banquet master has rooms full of magnificent robes that He is willing to give away so that all the guests can enjoy the feast. But people must be willing to take off their rags and put on the new clothes."

"Casy, my sister, I want to believe it, but" GB paused "how do I change my old ways of thinking? How can I become like a worm who becomes a moth?"

"Simple: by accepting that you can't do it alone. Sometimes, The Voice opens our wounds so He can heal them, just as a doctor sometimes breaks a bone to reset it properly. Sometimes we feel like we are dying in one way so we can live in another."

GB looked at his friend, standing erect, bright, and beaming with compassion.

"How do you do it, Casy? I mean, you are so strong and cheerful. You think about others despite your, er, disability." He felt awkward saying it so bluntly.

"I don't know, GB. I suppose I've grown accustomed to it and have been given the grace to accept what I can't change. Perhaps focusing on others helps me cope with my own issues. Everybody has something. No one gets off without a load to bear. I think I'm lucky because my issue is simple. It's much worse for people with broken hearts. That kind of pain is hard to pinpoint and even harder to live with."

"Agreed, big sister. Come on, let's get going! I'll put the finishing touches on the cart. We need to be gone before Seth comes. And, Casy, thanks for listening to my stuff. It helped me sort it out!"

[34]
NEW YORK CALLS

FROM THE TOP OF THE WATERFALL, Raan could see the upper branches of tall pines and the broad-leaf canopy of the forest below. A stone stairway descended along the cliff face to his left, and he vigorously sprang down it and was soon surrounded by trees. From below, the stairway was wholly hidden from sight, making it a perfect secret entrance to the castle.

The path wound on until it met a road. To the left, he could see the stone bridge leading to the castle gate; to the right, it curved down into the forest. Raan was so relieved to be free from the cavern that 'he'd thought little about what to do next. He was ready for this adventure to be over. He would have given the prince's treasure for a box of Oreos and a slice of pepperoni pizza.

What more can I do? he thought as he hiked down toward the road. But he thought about his friends, Barredoch and the greedy merchants, and the prince lying sick, paralyzed by hallucinating dreams. He figured that no one in town would believe his story, especially because of the rumor that he and Seth were at the center of a plot to gain the prince's fortune. He dearly wished that the men from the music shop would come and take him back.

On his right, he spied the glint of something through an opening in the trees; drawing closer, he saw a small pond, its surface like a mirror that reflected the sky and the tops of the surrounding trees. But his eyes were drawn to a bright, golden blob that slowly moved throughout the pond just under the surface. At first he thought it was a trick of the sun and clouds, so he walked to the 'water's edge, hoping for a better view. The orange-gold underwater mass changed shape and scintillated in the sunlight, darting one way, then another, and finally coming so close he could see, and then Raan laughed out loud:

"It's a school of goldfish swimming free in a pond in the woods. I wonder how they got here?"

The unexpected sight diffused all his tension, and he relaxed as the swarming blob swam into deeper water. Suddenly, right before him, the pond's mirrored surface became like a window, and Raan could see below. There were streets and sidewalks, taxis and pedestrians. He saw a taco cart and a street vendor hawking food, motioning him to come and eat. He saw a stairway leading to an ornate door with shining brass fixtures and a lavish doorknob.

"New York! Home! My front door!" an astonished Raan said aloud, knowing all he needed to do was walk down the stairs, and he'd be back home safe and snug in Manhattan. He had never felt so much love for his home before. Suddenly, he sincerely appreciated all of it: the crowds, the smell, the sounds, his cats, rude salespeople, and everything else. In all its glory and misery, New York was calling him back.

His thoughts returned to Casy, GB, Seth, the kindly prince, and all the misled townspeople. And considered the oppressed children who would be forced to work like animals if Barredoch and the silk barons had their way. Something stirred in him that made him think he couldn't abandon it all, so he turned away from the pond, deciding to live out this fantasy to whatever end. Then he realized this was the third danger: the temptation to doubt, to give up and take the easy path.

His will hardened, and Raan returned to the castle. On his way, he found a patch of edible mushrooms in the woods and filled his pockets. He found a way to climb the wall and return into his cell before being missed. That night, Raan substituted the healthy mushrooms he found in the forest for the poisoned ones in the kitchen, and Koal didn't suspect it and continued to feed the prince unpoisoned porridge. Raan hoped he'd be able to talk to Terrion soon and explain everything.

It had been six days since Raan left his friends, and he wondered if they would be worried, since he had not been able to send word. Now that he had a plan in motion, his hope grew. But he was still weak, and the dark passages were wearing on his nerves. Still, the prince improved quickly, and they began whispering together once the mushroom effect wore off. Raan explained what he had seen and heard about the Grand Protector and Koal's plans and confirmed he had received the message, but Terrion didn't remember sending it.

"Then who sent it and made the coded note?" said Raan, becoming more puzzled than ever.

"I think I know," said Terrion, but he was interrupted by a sound at the door. The prince sprang into bed, and Raan scrambled into a hiding place.

Two soldiers walked into the room and stood at a distance from the prince's bed.

"It's hard to see him like this," said the first.

"Master Koal said the prince's illness is very contagious and we should keep back twelve feet," said the second.

"I heard that he's delirious and might say anything . . ."

"Master Koal told the night watch that he had been talking nonsense, saying crazy things about conspiracies and poisoning attempts, and we shouldn't believe a word, no matter how sincere he sounds."

"And there's the one they have in the dungeon, the thief; he's crazy too, I hear. Olie said he sings nonsense when he's not sleeping."

"And says he's friends with the prince. It's a sad lot we have . . ."

The soldiers left, and Raan came from hiding and walked over to Terrion, sitting on the edge of his bed.

"Things are more complicated than I guessed," said Terrion, "Koal has poisoned the minds of my men too. It will be more difficult to prove Koal's deception while everyone thinks we're both out of our minds."

Raan thought about Seth, Casy, and GB and said, "I wish Seth were here; he always has wisdom."

"I wish my friend Zambo were here; he's the best at working miracles," said the prince.

"Zambo?" said Raan, thinking of the last line of the cryptic note. He remembered it reading, the king's servant Z. "Yes, we need a miracle," said Raan, reaching to the place on his chest where the stone used to hang on its string.

Quietly, Raan hastened back to the dungeon, listening for the sound of barefoot footsteps.

***

His strength returned within hours, and the prince began to move about, taking laps around his bedroom, stretching, and reviving stiff limbs. However, after each time, he would return to his bed, pretending to be sick, and wait until he became strong enough to confront Koal.

[35]
Conspiracy Discovered

ENSURING THERE WAS SOMEONE to care for the animals and plenty of fresh provisions for Seth, Casy and GB set out for the market with a cart of new apples pulled by Casy's donkey Lightening. After selling the entire load to one buyer, they zig-zagged their way through town, hoping to avoid being seen. Just as they reached the city gate, out stepped the listener with a rucksack on his back.

"Don't worry; I packed my own supplies." Seth grinned, clearly enjoying the look on Casy and GB's faces.

"You spoil all the fun!" said Casy playfully.

"You're late!" said GB, pretending to be annoyed. He and Casy looked at each other with a sigh, more of relief than anything.

"And here, GB," said Seth, handing a stout staff to the young Bibgit. "You never know when an iron-tipped walking stick could come in handy. Casy could beat off a wild boar with her crutch if needed. Most likely, she'd love it to death." Seth looked at the brave woman with a knowing smile.

"Come on and join the expedition!" Casy invited. "You're just looking for an excuse for a holiday."

"So what if I am," said the tall man. "I sure am due for one."

The older man walked as the two young people sat in the cart. GB held the reins and urged Lightning, their shaggy donkey onward. There was a lot of bumping and jostling on their two-day journey, but they enjoyed it as part of the fun. Yet as they neared the castle, they began to feel a sense of gloom. No one spoke, and the endless ranks of trees seemed like the pickets of an enormous fence hemming them in. The steady upward climb wore on their souls, and looking back, the downward slope beckoned them to turn around.

The night pressed, and the stillness breathed a hovering quiet where they could hear the soothing voice of the breeze and the whisper of leaves. As they sat around the fire waiting for sleep a horrific shriek pierced the night. Not too near, but not far enough away, thought Seth, noticing how the others quailed at the sound.

Seth threw a dead branch on the blaze. "The fire is friendly tonight. Thanks to GB's scrounging, we have enough wood to keep it going till morning. If it's clear tomorrow, we should see the castle towers glowing in the sunrise. Then, it's just a few hours, winding into the hills and over the bridge to the gate."

"What do you think we'll find?" Casy asked. "We have the note and the map, but a lot may have changed since they were written. Have you been to the castle?"

"A few times, officially, for prayers and dedications. Prince Terrion is a kind, clear-thinking man, but a little soft-hearted. He's lived alone since his family died during the great fever. We lost many." Seth paused, thoughtfully looked at Casy, and squeezed her hand gently, his gaze drifting toward the night sky.

Suddenly, another shriek followed by a howl rang through the darkness, causing everyone to cringe.

[36]

Under An Ocean of Stars

"Let me tell you a story," ventured Seth, who seemed as alarmed as the others.

The Listener settled into storyteller mode as the others got comfortable. GB threw dry branches on the fire, and in his musical voice, Seth began:

Dusk fell, and the last wedges of daylight peeked over the temple wall while deep lines of shadow grew in the outer courts. The inner sanctuary was bathed in the cool tones of twilight as Hochi busied himself trimming and refilling lamps in the House of Hearing. Hochi was approaching thirty but still had the healthy complexion and thick hair of youth. He had a curious mind and generous heart and took his work in the temple seriously. Aromas of burnt offerings lingered as fading smoke wafted around gigantic columns. It was the end of the day, and people were leaving.

There was still a group murmuring in intense discussion. Occasionally, a single voice rose above the rest in emotion and then died away, followed by the ringing questions of an adolescent boy. Hochi moved closer to get a better view.

He saw a lad of about twelve surrounded by a dozen or more temple men in flowing roles that Hochi had seen before. It was a humorous contrast: the deep-lined faces of the graybeards against the ruddy skin of the youth. The boy looked like a tradesman's apprentice, but his manner was calm and respectful, and his eyes were intense. The boy would ask a question, and then the men would debate over the answer.

As the night deepened, Hochi busied himself with his caretaker duties, refilling and trimming lamps, all the while wondering how a young boy could be there in the first place. Even though the lad looked like a tradesman's son, he assumed the child must be the child of a Listener or patron who'd come to visit for the day. A few more times he walked near enough to hear some of the conversation and realized that the boy was leading the discussion in the way only the wisest do.

Eventually the men began to leave, each elder assuming the lad belonged to someone else, until the boy was left alone with Hochi watching in the lamplight. The lad lifted both arms and began softly chanting until he noticed Hochi standing nearby, awkwardly entranced.

"They've all gone," the boy said as his eyes swept the hall. The lad turned and faced Hochi. "Will you be headed home, too?"

Hochi said, "I work here and was going to ask you the same question. Where is your family? Are you alone?"

"I'm never alone, especially in the House of the Voice," was His reply. "My parents will meet me here; I must wait for them."

The night air turned cold, and Hochi noticed a shiver in his young companion.

"Do you have a place to stay?" he queried.

"I must stay in this house. There are still many questions to ask tomorrow. My parents will know where to find me when they come."

Hochi felt perplexed; the boy was alone but seemed perfectly calm. The lad followed him to an alcove where a charcoal fire was burning. In its warmth and under lamplight, they talked through the night, eating food left over from the day's feasting. Hochi sometimes caught himself dozing, and the boy prayed with him and for him, seeming like a tireless warrior priest in a twelve-year-old body.

At dawn, Hochi's shift ended. He watched as the boy stood facing the sunrise, chanting adorations with his arms stretched to the horizon. Hochi returned home for a wash and a hearty breakfast, wondering if he should report the lost boy to the house guard.

***

Later that day, the hurried, slapping scrapes of sandaled feet echoed in the temple courtyard. A wide-eyed couple ignored the majestic buildings because their sense of awe was overwhelmed by panic—their child was missing.

The breathless parents froze in their steps when they saw the boy. Shaken by their intense search, they stared, wondering why they hadn't looked in the House of Hearing sooner. Then, they rushed to the boy, embracing him in a mix of joy and anger.

As the family left to join the other travelers headed north, the lad walked alongside his careworn parents. He apologized for causing his footsore mom and dad so much stress and thanked them for searching for him.

They eagerly listened to his stories and then noticed the lad was famished.

The mother called for a halt, and they enjoyed bread dipped in olive oil and spices. The travel food strengthened them, and they returned to the road eager for progress. The boy carried much of his mother's load, and the threesome plodded through the miles with hopeful hearts, knowing they'd be home in less than a week.

The campsite where they stopped was dotted with cooking fires scattered across the darkening landscape. The boy savored the rich aroma of fresh bread and felt his belly growl. Quickly, his dad had a fire going, and the little family was soon feasting and talking about everything they had experienced over the past few days.

The fire's warmth and twilight calm seeped into their tired limbs. The youth began to sing. Softly at first, but as he grew louder, the entire campground of many families grew quiet, listening closely to catch a whisper of the beautiful melody that felt distant yet near the heart.

The song ended, and an incredible stillness came over the camp. It was as if the night air applauded with sounds only heard by the stars.

The mother looked at her son's face, and the boy looked back. His deep brown eyes glinted in the firelight. Without a word, his gaze said, "I see you and understand, and everything will turn out okay." The tired woman relaxed and smiled as if a heavy weight had been lifted from her shoulders. She saw the son she had nursed and comforted as a baby; she knew now that the boy could comfort her.

The last thing she remembered before sleep took her was the lad's compassionate face looking out over the sleeping travelers under an ocean of stars.

Seth, Casy, and GB all sat quietly, almost dozing in that wonderful liminal place of almost asleep. Like statues or a beautiful painting, they waited, present but invisible, set aglow by the waning firelight.

I must die so a new story can be born in me. My dreams of glory, power, and influence must perish for it to come to life. I take the leap of faith, knowing there is no turning back, expecting nothing but the reward of a place at the table of Holy Love.
(From the Journals of Zambo the Mute)

[37]

ATTACKED!

THE DAY DAWNED FAIR, and the travelers were up with the sun. Its early rays melted away the dewdrops, and GB stirred the embers of the fire and got a small blaze going to ward off the chill. They saw no sign of whatever creature had made the uncanny shriek during the night. As Seth predicted, they could see the castle's turrets peeking over the treetops between two hills. They hoped they would be greeted by Raan and the prince and learn the reason for the riddling note, but their expectations ran afoul when they were greeted by someone they didn't expect.

***

Koal and Conga were out early on their morning walk. They played fetch, and Conga panted hard, chasing a well chewed stick with zeal and ferocity, encouraged by Koal, who constantly teased the dog into a frenzy. The two were in a fierce tug-of-war when the friends came around a corner, singing and laughing gaily. The hound was spooked in the middle of a snarl, and Koal yelled in surprise, which sparked the animal to attack!

The colossal dog charged the friends at full speed. Casy and GB watched as the savage wolfhound bore down on Seth as he walked alongside the wagon. Seth stiffened, expecting the worst, calling, "Whoa, big guy!" and reached his palm forward, hoping to slow the beast.

His face was white with terror, but he managed to put on a calm façade as the charging animal approached. The beast's front teeth bit through Seth's shirt, gripped his forearm, and stopped as if holding its prey, waiting for orders.

Seth stood motionless with the skin of his arm gripped in a bite just strong enough to say, I've got you; if you move, I'll rip your arm off.

"You've got a well-trained watchdog, Koal. I'd appreciate it if you'd call it off. It's hard to say hello while distracted," said Seth, calmly bluffing, trying to sound in control while knowing his arm was no match for the jaws of the massive wolfhound.

"Call it off!" yelled Casy, bristling.

Koal looked at Casy, stunned by the fire in her eyes as she stood in the cart, surveying the scene. She and Koal locked eyes, but Koal couldn't hold her gaze long and looked down.

"Call it off now!" said Casy.

As Koal delayed, the tension mounted. Seth held himself motionless but felt a tickle in his throat beginning to nag. He fought the instinct as long as he could, but finally, a muted cough escaped his lips, his body jerking slightly. Instantly, the dog bit deep into Seth's forearm, and in a violent reflex, Seth wrenched away, and the dog's teeth ripped his arm open to the bone. The beast snarled and prepared to strike again, and Seth stumbled backward, fell, hit his head on the wagon, and blacked out. The wolfhound pounced on the unconscious man, but just as it opened its jaws to go for the throat, a leaping GB brought the iron-tipped staff solidly on the dog's head. The hound went limp.

"My dog!" Koal called as he ran to the wagon, pulling the animal's body away from Seth.

"Seth!" cried Casy and GB. Casy jumped out of the wagon, landed on her weak foot, and buckled in pain, wincing as she crawled to her dad, looking at the massive cut and the white bone contrasting with the pink and yellowish flesh flowing with red. Another stream of blood coursed from a gash on Seth's head.

"Have mercy on us!" GB prayed as he knelt beside the unconscious man.

Casy began to tear strips of cloth from her dress. "Hurry, GB. Push both sides of the cut together and hold them steady," said Casy in a confident, calm voice.

"I got this," said GB and gently but firmly pressed the unconscious man's open gash together while Casy used her improvised bandages to wrap and immobilize Seth's right arm.

"I didn't mean for it to go that far. It was just a joke," Koal blurted with empty excuses. "Conga is hard to control when he gets excited. He was just being a dog."

"You mean doing what you taught him to do," said GB as he kept his eyes on Seth.

"That dog's a weapon!" said Casy without looking up, holding back tears and working on bandaging Seth's head. "Come on, help us lift him into the cart. We'll get him to the castle."

So Koal and GB lifted Seth into the back of the cart, and they all followed Koal back to the castle courtyard. They laid Seth on a bench, and Koal instructed servants to heat water and bring more bandages.

That morning Raan was hidden atop the castle wall basking unseen in the morning sun when he saw the friends arrive. Seeing Seth's condition, he quickly ran to his unconscious friend.

Koal was stunned. "Where did you come from? I thought you—"

"Thought what? That I was trapped in the dungeon?" said Raan angrily, kneeling next to Seth, assessing his wounded arm and head, then looking at Casy and a bewildered GB.

Just then, several of the prince's soldiers came running.

"What happened here? Be swift!" said the captain.

"What's happening is that Koal had been poisoning the prince for weeks and has kept him in bed, sick with tainted food!" said Raan earnestly.

"What's this?" asked the captain.

"You lie," jeered Koal.

"That's too easy a word for you," returned Raan.

"First, we must tend to the injured man," said the captain. "We'll sort the rest out later."

With Seth being cared for by the prince's men, Casy refocused on the fact that Raan was alive and saying unbelievable things.

"Prince Terrion has been bedridden by a slow poison, courtesy of Koal. He and the Grand Protector are plotting to seize control of Terrion's power and fortune."

"That's nonsense!" said Koal, seeing his plan unraveling and glancing side to side like a cornered beast. Eying the open gate, he started to make a break for it when a colossal voice bellowed from above, stopping him in his tracks.

[38]
Treachery Exposed

"WHAT'S ALL THIS? I'm sure we can work it out in everyone's favor!" said the voice of Barredoch.

Surprisingly, the enormous man swaggered on a narrow catwalk that spanned two towers directly over the courtyard. He spoke with the authoritative voice he always used to take control. Where did he come from, wondered Raan.

"Don't listen to him! He'll trick us all!" Casy shouted from the side of her wounded dad. Seth tried to stand but fell back in a heap.

"I forgive you for everything," said the Grand Protector in an injured but benevolent tone. "Even your rebellion against me and my loving son can be excused because it's all been a big misunderstanding."

"What an actor," said Raan. "He makes it sound as if everything is our fault."

"A rebellion against a rebel! If you call bringing justice and uncovering corruption a rebellion, so be it!" said GB defiantly.

"What do you know about justice, impudent brat?" roared the Grand Protector contemptuously.

"What right does justice have to speak to corruption? Every right!" said GB, brimming with passion.

"Corruption? Your books are no more than fairy tales and superstitions to control the weak-minded!" said the Grand Protector, bordering on rage.

With an agonizing effort, Seth rose to his feet and spoke in a clear, calm voice: "One who has not tasted the apple cannot know its sweetness! You say our minds are weak, but we don't need any genius to see through your schemes. Let's talk about it, man to man. You can't imagine all that is going on. You might realize that you're the one who doesn't understand."

"How would you know what I imagine or understand?" said Barredoch in a rage that shook the catwalk. "You religious people are always ready to condescend."

"We don't condescend; we stand level with you, looking up. I'm the neediest of all. Even now, the strong arm of love invites you. Why do you spit on the hand that reaches out to help? Why torment yourself? Forgiveness is generous—forgiveness is a gift. We all come begging bread, and He gives us a banquet."

The catwalk swayed as the Grand Protector paused, not knowing what to say, as if an inner debate battled within him. For an instant his face softened, but slowly hardness regained mastery. Barredoch said loudly, "I'd spit on its hand and slap it in the face. I have no use for ghost stories and softhearted sentimentality or pity. The world doesn't run on love; it runs on domination and the backs of fools."

"You're wrong," said Seth, reaching out to steady himself. "Love empowers the world despite those who vainly strive to control it by fear. People who live in love propel the world forward through the gifts of joy, regardless of those trapped in greed and lust for power!"

Suddenly, as if struck by an invisible club, Seth slumped back in dizzying pain, and Casy stooped to comfort him.

Unexpectedly, a new voice trumpeted above the din: "Enough of this deception, brother! Your treachery is exposed!"

Everyone looked up, and there, tall upon the catwalk opposite the Grand Protector, stood Prince Terrion. He was thin and pale, yet erect in his royal robes, and full of regal confidence. His gray eyes were noble and alert, radiating indomitable justice, beaming with compassion.

"Brother?" said Raan, stunned seeing the prince revealed in majesty.

Koal spat and started to say something, but GB gave him such a fierce look that the tall boy stepped back and held his tongue.

"Why these plots, brother? You have everything you need," said Terrion with generous compassion.

"Everything?" said the Grand Protector. "Everything you say I need, but not all I want. Father gave me the town. But all I do all day is listen to complaints and make decisions for people who can't think for themselves. Father gave you the land, title, and treasure, and you perch here in your castle; you save yourself for the big ideas while I slog along in everyday grit."

The big man stepped toward the prince, and the catwalk swayed.

"But it's my turn now," said Barredoch, fuming uncontrollably, rushing the prince, and the two men grappled on the narrow bridge.

Barredoch grabbed the prince's throat, but Terrion broke his grip. The Grand Protector reached for a hidden knife, but the prince forced Barredoch's wrist against one of the ropes, and the Grand Protector winced and dropped the weapon. Locked hand in hand, the brothers strove as the catwalk swayed. The frenzied Grand Protector pressed his greater bulk upon his weaker brother, and Terrion bent under the weight. It didn't look good for the prince, weakened by the poison, and his soldiers raced up the stairs in support, but before they reached the battling men, the brothers lost their balance and fell, crashing in a tangle of arms and legs on the pavement below.

[39]
ESCAPE?

KOAL PUSHED PAST RAAN and GB and knelt beside the twisted body of his dad. A pool of blood began to form under the big man's skull. There was no breath, no heartbeat; the big man's body was still. The prince's soldiers ran to the body of their lord, and the servants stood ready.

Suddenly GB said, "Look at the prince; he's moving!"

Everyone noticed as the prince's left hand lifted slowly and shakily, pointing directly at Raan. His other hand slipped into the folds of his jacket as if trying to grip something, but then Prince Terrion died. There was a tender pause as everyone waited. A flock of sparrows darted in and around the castle courtyard and flew up and over the wall. The sun drew low, and long shadows carved into bright spaces, threatening the coming night. Raan's heart was heavier than ever. Everyone was overwhelmed with grief—except one.

Koal stood up and said, "The prince is dead. My father, the prince's brother, is dead. That makes me the new prince!" Straightening to his full height, he pronounced, "I'm the rightful heir! I claim the title; bow to me, my subjects!"

No one bowed, and everyone started talking at once, sending the courtyard into mayhem.

I've failed, thought Raan. Evil has won. Raan sank to his knees, his mind swirling, wondering why 'he'd been sent on this adventure—all for what?

He cried aloud to the Voice he barely knew, "How can this be? Won't you help us?"

"Crying to your invisible fairy tale can't help you now. I'm in charge here," said Koal.

"That will need to be verified," spoke the resonant voice of Seth, sitting straight, looking grim and blood-soaked but very much alive.

"There might be a will," said Casy.

"You'll have to prove he was in his right mind," said Koal.

"Are you ready to admit you've been slowly feeding the prince poison food for weeks?" said Raan, not ready to give up either.

"I admit nothing!" Koal shot back. We'll see who the townspeople believe: their beloved Grand Protector's son, who is now the rightful prince, or you, a cracked group of religious fanatics. It's your story against mine." Koal edged toward the castle gate, thinking he could bribe or threaten the servants and soldiers who had heard everything. He ran for the open gate, dashing past Raan and GB and sprinting toward the stables through the stone arch.

"Quick, catch him! If he gets to town first, he'll spread lies and rumors and twist the whole thing in his favor," shouted Casy.

Raan and GB sprang after Koal but suddenly heard a horrible scream followed by a gurgling, deep-throated shriek that made their blood run cold. They raced to the gate only to see the back of the gigantic Chimera dragging the twitching body of Koal into the trees.

"I'm going to be sick," said GB, looking for a corner.

Raan sprinted after the creature, not knowing what he could do. Crazy or brave, he chased the retreating beast, and in a small clearing, he found the Chimera brooding over its prey. His stomach turned as he watched the mountain demon feed. The creature looked up, yellow-eyed, leering. Raan stood resolute, and after some long seconds, staring eye to eye with the beast, the Chimera looked down, seized its victim's arm in its beak, and dragged the body deeper into the underbrush.

There was a long silence; Raan couldn't think straight, so he stared into the trees until two of Terrion's men found him and said, "Sir, come quickly, the prince. There's something you should see."

Dreamlike, Raan passed under the arch of the castle gate and joined his friends. He saw Casy, Seth, and GB staring in shock and speechless, and then, as if on cue, they all looked at the prince's body.

"His left hand is still pointing to where you were standing, but his right hand is reaching for something in his shirt," said Casy excitedly.

They knelt next to the nobleman's fallen body and found an envelope. One of the soldiers reached to retrieve it and reverently handed it to his commander.

The captain noticed the gold, embossed seal and said, "Now is not the time or place to open this. I'll keep it safe. First, we must tend to the fallen. Come, let's do what must be done."

The prince's soldiers and servants tended to the bodies of Terrion and Barredoch, and the two brothers were laid side by side in the castle's main hall. A search for the body of Koal only revealed a mangled shoe and a long knife without a sheath. They were placed next to the bodies of his kinsmen.

With that business finished, swift riders were sent to the king and townspeople to deliver the tragic news and ask for counsel. As the riders rode away, Raan looked around the courtyard and saw a thin, gray-bearded man standing quietly in the shadows. He was momentarily distracted, and when he looked back, the figure had vanished.

[40]
ZAMBO

THE FRIENDS STAYED SEVERAL nights in the castle and planned to head home when Seth was well enough to travel.

As they took their last meal, Casy said, "Something is bugging me. If the prince was sick with Koal's mushrooms, how could he write the coded note, create the map, and arrange to have it delivered without Koal finding out?"

"Maybe he wrote it before he got sick and slipped it to the farmers when they passed the castle on a delivery," said GB.

"Possibly," said Raan, who wondered how the men from the music shop came to be the prince's messengers, "but you remember that I ate the poisoned mushrooms and was immediately affected. There is no way I could have done it, even after one dose of the drug. The prince was poisoned for days."

Seth smiled and said, "I think we have the answer, but we didn't see it at first." He pulled the cryptic letter from his bag, showed it to his friends, and pointed to the last word, the single letter Z. "I think the Z stands for Zambo."

"Zambo?" the three said in unison.

"Yes, Zambo the Mute, the prince's trusted friend and servant. He's the hermit I mentioned before and lives near this castle. He's a very great person but a wisp of a man. He's so tall and thin that you might think the slightest wind would blow him away. His ingenuity is legendary, so a coded puzzle would be easy for him."

"Maybe we should have gotten Zambo to help us," said Casy.

"I don't think he would have, at least in a way that we'd like. Zambo is kind and good but does things his own way and keeps his distance," said Seth with a far-off look, as if he were trying to penetrate the unusual thoughts and motives of the hermit.

"I think I may have seen him," said Raan. "I'm not sure—but when I crawled from the river after my fight with the Chimera, I was exhausted and without any direction. I saw two feet in the dense fog, and they guided me to the castle gate. They disappeared as soon as I touched the front steps. Other times, I thought I heard footsteps in the dark passages, but they sounded as if they were avoiding me, trying not to be discovered."

"I'm curious to meet him," said GB.

"Can we try to find him? I have so many questions," said Casy.

Seth said, "He lives alone in a small cottage in the forest near here. We should try to see if he's home."

When they found the cottage, the hermit wasn't there. The front door was left ajar, as if to say, Come in. So the friends entered and respectfully looked around. There were cases of books, a drawing table, a work bench, and a small kitchen with simple cooking gear. The fireplace was cold, so the friends assumed that Zambo had been away for days. But lying on the table was an envelope labeled "Raan."

"How did he know my name?" thought Raan aloud, and then to himself he thought, All this is connected. I wish I could put it together.

"Open it! What does it say?" said Casy, unable to contain herself.

"Indeed, Raan, if you don't mind, I'm very curious," said Seth, stepping behind the lad so he could see better.

Raan opened the note and read aloud:

> "Thank you for saving my friend. Well done! Sadly, there were some who would not be saved. For them, I'm grieved. You have one adventure left and one responsibility. I'm forbidden to help directly, but I'm allowed to give clues. You already have what you need, but here is the clue that will help you start. Z"

Included with the note was the picture of a shield that contained a coat of arms.

[41] An Angry Mob

THE WEATHER ON THE JOURNEY down the mountain was cloudy, and the view of the road swam with patches of low mist that were sometimes wet enough to dampen their faces. None of the friends had much to say and remained lost in their own thoughts. They all desired to get home, eat a hot meal, and rest their feet in front of a blazing fireplace.

As the companions came into town, an angry mob barred their way. Hundreds of townspeople and Bibgits swarmed the friends. Some were friends with Barredoch and the Qerds, others were farmers, craftspeople, and weavers who were tired of corruption and threats of violence. There were also Bibgits whose anger was boiling over because of the townspeople's prejudice toward them. Others were swept up in the excitement of the crowd and only wanted to learn the news. The mob pressed in, and everyone wanted to blame someone for how miserable they felt.

Rumors had been spreading about what happened at the castle, but no one knew the full story. Many were hostile toward the Listener because they believed the lies Barredoch and the Qerds spread. Others knew of Seth's selfless work in the community, his kindness, and his noble life. The Bibgits laughed at both groups because they considered their arguments petty. A standoff developed between all factions, and tensions reached their breaking point.

Faces glared, livid from years of frustration with the corrupt administration. Still others were caught up in the mob's confusion and became consumed by a frenzy for revenge. Raan and his friends became the target.

One angry villager shouted, "How could anyone allow this kind of tragedy?"

A large man, red-faced with a bushy beard named Blemósh, boldly stepped forward. Raan recognized him as one of the Qerds blackmailing Barredoch. He planted his long walking stick in the ground before him and loudly said, "What's all this?" Several other mean-looking men stepped forward in support. "As Deputy Grand Protector, I demand an explanation!"

"The Grand Protector is dead!" cried another voice from the crowd. "We're tired of all his corruption!"

"And his heavy-handed thugs!" called another from a group of stout farmers pushing to the front of the crowd.

The Deputy Grand Protector spat and yelled, "It's their fault!" Pointing at the friends.

Angry people crowded the cart, and it looked like they would seize Seth and Raan. But then another voice called:

"We've had enough of you townsfolk treating us like second-class slaves!" shouted Kia, stepping up with two-dozen hardened Bibgits with drawn bows.

It seemed like a brawl was about to erupt when Seth stood and gestured with his upraised hand so everyone would be silent.

"Let him speak!" said a voice.

"What do you have to say for yourself?" shouted another.

Seth remained calm and waited for the people to settle.

"We all know this dance," said Seth, "and when the music changes, we need to adjust. If we don't bend, we'll break. The key to getting through times when the future seems dark is faith."

"What's he talking about?" asked a woman with a child on her hip.

"We don't want no religious nonsense," said a gruff man in a tattered hat.

"Let him speak," said another.

Seth continued, "We can have faith in many things: ourselves, our friends, our way of life; and we also can have faith in the Voice, and that surpasses all. Wherever you put your faith, you need it now. As we strengthen our faith, we become wiser. And with wisdom, the worries and fears that confuse us will shrink, allowing us to overcome them. We will overcome together!"

People pricked up their ears and drew closer. Seth stood humbly above them. He leaned on GB's staff, weary but alive in the Spirit. He called out, "Yet with every change, there is new territory to explore. And with new territories come new treasures, new battles, and unexpected enemies—foes that are sometimes bigger and stronger than we are. We must learn to fight with new weapons. With the weapons of trust and persistence, we can harness the power of love. With those tools of warfare, we will outlast our foes, the real enemies—fear and confusion."

"What weapons are you talking about?" said one of the Qerds.

Several Bibgits gripped their bows and stepped forward. Kia held his breath.

Seth lifted his voice again, wincing in pain. "The battle can be won only by trusting each other, seeking truth, and persisting with a humble desire to listen. And know this one sure thing . . ." Seth paused to emphasize this last point with the remainder of his strength. "Our battles are only lost when we stop fighting. We will prevail if we stand together and honor those we've lost."

Blood was beginning to soak through the bandages on his head and arm, and red drops started to fall onto the sideboard of the cart. Seth tottered so much that Casy handed him her crutch. The Listener continued, thinking it might be his last sermon: "We can encourage each other by example, service, sacrifice, and love, and instead of separating, join with the unfailing belief that everyone, no matter what creed or tribe, has value."

Seth coughed, and Raan supported him while handing him a mug of water. The Listener was determined to finish, so he waved the water off and continued in a raspy voice, "When we trust one another, the strongholds of fear are shattered, and we can confidently say it will be okay!"

His voice grew in intensity.

"This is because faith releases power and the strength to persevere. When we persevere, our deeds become a beam of hope that shatters darkness; the battle continues, but joy and hope cannot be overcome."

Seth picked up the pace with a last effort. "Where dark cannot dominate, it corrupts; when corruption fails, it confuses; when confusion is defeated, darkness brings doubt. But in the plain, simple light of day, doubt is banished—and truth illuminates the glory of each man or woman that stands with it. We can go on together!"

Seth slumped, and Raan caught him and eased him to the seat. The people were silent, united in thought until someone shouted out:

"Very fine words you have, but we've been listening to the Grand Protector's empty words for years. What makes what you say any different? We need something more!" Said an older townsperson speaking for many.

Seth looked over the crowd. His head pounded, and his weak legs and arms trembled from blood loss and trauma. Still he remained unmoving, like a rough-cut statue carved out of living humanity waiting for the chisel.

"Look everyone! Look at the light!" Casy said.

A clear mist shimmered above the crowd and then slowly began to envelop each person in a ghostly aura."

"I see it too, Casy," said GB. "What is it? It's not sunbeams. It seems like it's coming from inside each person."

Everyone saw it—a glowing sheen as if they were all lit from within. No matter what they believed, everyone saw a shimmering light from everyone around them, but no one understood it.

The people called out, "What is it, Listener? Strange lightning, a trick of yours, a mountain demon's spell?"

"It's not the weather of this world and no trick of mine or spell. Be still and wait. The Voice is showing us that there is good in every man, woman, and child."

Some were afraid, others curious, others angry because they couldn't control it, but everyone waited, wondering what would happen next.

Unable to hold back his curiosity, Raan touched Casy's shoulder, and his glow mingled with hers, creating a beautiful dancing glimmer that connected them. People saw what happened and began to touch those standing near them, and soon the whole crowd was bathed in dancing, flowing radiance.

Suddenly Casy shouted, "It's beginning to rain! It feels so warm and clean."

Rain. Steady, gentle, windless rain, warm and secure, came. It lightly fell on their heads and clothes, seeping into the ground. They were soaked through, but no one moved or spoke. Each man and woman, young and old, townsfolk, Qerd, and Bibgit, quietly waited while the cleansing shower covered them.

A woman with her face turned to the sky called out, "I feel like my grief is being washed away."

"It's like a heavy load is sliding off my back," said an old workman, feeling the water running down his upturned cheeks.

"I feel like dancing," said a mother holding a baby, turning a little jig where she stood.

"I haven't felt this happy in years," said a young Qerd, cracking a smile from ear to ear.

One by one, the people experienced the release of burdens, worries, fears, and doubts as the years of oppression melted away and their hearts became free.

Raan spoke quietly, "And who could know, here we are, washed in the tears of heaven's joy."

Casy heard him and looked into his eyes as streams flowed from hers. GB stood in silent reverence, his head bowed and hands raised. Seth raised his eyes as water droplets ran through his gray-brown hair. He looked over the vast array of faces, sighing a deep sigh of contentment. His loving smile was filled with peace. He quietly spoke:

"This is real enough for me, thank you!"

[42]
Turning Tables

THE ENVELOPE WITH Terrion's golden seal was his will, and it was read in the presence of the king's ambassadors and the town council; Raan was astonished to learn he was given everything: property, title, and fortune. A great town meeting was held. Everyone's stories were told, and a narrative was written that would serve as a record of the truth. In the telling, Raan relived his painful time in the darkness and his uncanny encounter with the Voice. Others came forward to tell stories of the abusive things the Grand Protector and Qerds had done to them, no longer needing to remain silent for fear. Everyone who had something to say was heard. It was a long, patient process, but finally, everything that needed to be said was said, and the people went to their homes satisfied they had been heard.

Two days later, Raan called Seth, GB and Casy, Kia, Emma, and a few other town leaders, and the king's envoys together for a private meeting. Emma turned out to be very helpful and was exceptionally good at organizing and taking notes, so Raan made her his assistant.

"Thank you all for taking the time to join me. I've been thinking about how the silk barons and Qerd leaders tried to turn the people of our land into bondslaves. It's only a matter of time before they try again."

"If not here, they will try somewhere else," interrupted Emma. Her disruption was excused partially because of her sweet grandmotherly disposition and also because she had provided the meeting with an enormous batch of koluchka and other sweets.

Raan continued, "Well said, Emma, we shouldn't think only of ourselves but of the other lands around us. We must stop these corrupt businesses must be stopped if we can. I've invited Corrigan and Dalmone, the King's envoys, to help with this because it concerns royal law. I have a plan that may put an end to the illegal silk trafficking . . ."

Raan explained his plan to the group, and they all agreed. "Now we must wait for the prey to walk into our trap," said Raan. So they patiently waited until one day the Qerd named Blemósh approached Raan as he was walking home.

"I have some friends who would enjoy the honor of meeting you, about a matter of importance that may be to your advantage," said Blemósh in a low voice.

"Of course," said Raan, "I'd be happy to meet them. They can set up a time with Emma, my assistant."

"Well, my friends are rather shy and would appreciate the meeting going, shall we say, unnoticed," said Blemósh, with a wink.

"I see," said Raan, with his eyes half closed as if he were contemplating. "Tell them ten o'clock next Tuesday night, at the Grand Protector's office. The town will be quiet then."

"Very good, I'll tell them," said Blemósh. He turned down a side street and was gone.

Ten o'clock Tuesday night arrived, and Raan was sitting behind his desk when the same elegant ebony carriage, drawn by two horses, parked in front of the side door to the Grand Protector's office. A pair of large tapers burned brightly on his desktop, flickering playfully on the walls, and a newly installed black velvet curtain spanned one outside wall, hiding the outer windows from view. Raan calmly watched as the three men he'd seen before swaggered into the office. They were followed by a sheepish Blemósh and the Qerds that had blackmailed Barredoch. These three remained near the door.

"Welcome gentlemen, please make yourselves comfortable." said Raan as he motioned to several chairs sitting opposite him. "What can I do for you?"

"Perhaps, what we can do for you will be more interesting," said the man with a large ring and sinister voice, placing a stack of gold coins on the desk just as before.

Raan didn't flinch and calmly said, "What do you mean?"

"Let's come to the point. I appreciate that in a leader. Even one as young as your honorable self will understand the financial potential that is open before you," said the man.

"Go on," said Raan.

"Several forward-thinking leaders of other districts have agreed that the quaint methods of silk manufacture and distribution in this country are outdated and that reforms are needed."

"What kind of reforms?" asked Raan.

"For one, the centralized manufacture and standardized sale of all silk products. The new streamlined, efficient operation would be under your control. Did we say you will be rewarded with a portion of the profits for your astute stewardship? Several other wise community leaders are already becoming quite wealthy through this arrangement."

"These lands belong to the king. What does he think about this plan?" said Raan carefully. "He taxes each farmer and weaver based on what they can afford, and both the king and people benefit. It is a fair arrangement that gives the farmers and artisans the freedom to create the most beautiful silk products in the kingdom."

"The king doesn't need to know about our little arrangement, and it is easy to persuade the king's tax collectors with incentives," the man said with a wink. "You can allow some artisans to continue as before, paying taxes as usual, while most of the silk is sold to us tax free. Did we say that you, as this district's progressive leader, get part of the profits? Tax free."

"I think that we've heard enough," said a stern voice, and Corrigan and Dalmone, the king's envoys, stepped from behind the curtain with four soldiers. Blemósh and the Qerds tried to dash through the door, but more soldiers blocked their escape.

"They will have a lot of explaining to do at the court," said Dalmone as the soldiers led the merchants away.

"Thank you for your help, Raan, er, Prince and Grand Protector. We couldn't have caught them without you," said Corrigan.

"You're welcome, I'm glad to help," said Raan. "Thank you for clearing this up. Our people will continue to be free to farm and create as they choose and make this part of the king's realm a center of beauty and joy."

Raan felt relieved as the king's envoys rode off. He walked home alone. It was a clear night, and stars hung shimmering in a sable sky. The last aura of day still clung to the edge of the horizon in a faint line of violet, and then he watched it disappear, leaving him in the sole company of the grand expanse of the heavens. It was breathtaking.

He walked on, taking a slow deep breath and feeling his body relax. At least that part of the mission is finished, he thought. Prince Terrion has passed on to his afterlife, so there is no more I can do for him. What's left of my mission? He wondered if the men from the Music Emporium would come to take him home. He unconsciously reached for the stone seeking the wisdom it had provided so many times and found an empty place on his chest. Then he thought about the Voice and said in a whisper, "Voice, are you there? Will you speak to me?"

"I am never far, but you often can't hear me," said a quiet voice so close to him as if it was next to his ear.

"Why not?" asked Raan, both surprised and delighted.

"There are many things that get in the way, good things and distracting things. Loud, noisy, and exciting things; kind intentions, noble thoughts, and some not so noble; worries, doubts, and ideas about the future; annoyances and complaints, there are many things. But mostly, you can't hear me because you don't want to."

Taken aback, Raan said, "I want to hear you now."

"That's good because I want to talk to you," said the Voice. "You have one task, and one adventure left to complete. Here's what you need to do ..."

[43]

Waters of One

RAAN WENT TO VISIT the Qerd families and learned that once the Qerd leaders in league with the merchants and Barredoch were apprehended, the other Qerds became completely different. It turned out, by nature, the Qerds were very nice and loved games and fun, but they wanted so much to please they could be easily misled. Without wicked leaders, they became willing to help anyone in need, anytime.

After meeting with the Qerds, Raan arranged meetings with the Bibgits, followed by meetings with the townspeople, artisans, and farmers. Once he'd spoken with each group, he called for an open meeting for all in the town square.

The morning sun was bright, and the sky was clear when the people gathered on the lawn before the town hall to hear Raan speak. Raan's back was to the building and before him an expanse of people stood. To his right, there were ten individuals standing solemnly, and to his left was a stone pillar about three feet high, topped with a large stone bowl.

In the crowd stood dozens of Bibgits, scores of townspeople peacefully assembling that were curious and attentive. There was a group of people experiencing severe hardship that Casy brought in her cart. Many farmers, artisans, and tradespeople gathered in groups eager to hear what the new prince would say. A group of Qerds also came at the invitation of Raan, who promised they would have a fresh start. Some of the Qerds looked skeptical, knowing how much terror they had caused as minions of the Grand Protector. Many of the people also looked skeptical, as some glanced sideways at the Qerds standing among them. Now we will see if the people will really embrace equality and forgiveness, thought Raan, hoping his plan would work.

Raan lifted a hand, and the crowd became silent.

"Welcome everyone! I congratulate each of you for your faithful use of your skills and talents for the good of our land and everyone who lives here. Thank you for treating others as you'd like to be treated."

Raan paused briefly and looked at a piece of paper he had in his pocket, and the people looked at each other as the kind words reached their hearts. They were not used to being appreciated and wondered if there was a catch.

"We stand together as heroes of our community, strong and able, wise and creative, hard-working and determined. I consider it a privilege to stand before you today!"

A single person began to clap tentatively and slowly more people joined until the applause rose into a sound like a rain shower but died away when Raan lifted his hand. Raan felt uncomfortable in the limelight but continued despite his awkwardness.

"I thank you for your commitment to our land the desire to work together, but I foresee that we will have challenges."

Seth and Emma, and many others, leaned in to hear better, and it was so quiet you could hear a pin drop.

Raan continued, "To help with these challenges, our leaders and I have created a new team called the Guardians of Unity. The Guardians will ensure that everyone involved in a dispute will have the right to speak their full story while the other person listens. Both sides of an issue will get equal attention. It's not the Guardians' role to judge or give advice but merely facilitate the discussion to allow both sides to be heard. The goal is to assure that each person in a dispute can share their point of view respectfully and completely."

Raan looked at the group of people standing on his right and continued, "Many cases will be complicated, but starting with each person's understanding of the other's perspective will go a long way to promote peace among us. The Guardians will ensure that everyone in the disagreement is willing to say, 'I want to understand your side of the story and hope I can learn something.' It is always true that both perspectives have great value, regardless of the situation."

Raan paused to glance at his paper and went on, "No system is perfect, but with the assistance of the Guardians of Unity, people will have hope knowing that they will have the chance to have their story heard in an atmosphere of respect."

Raan took a step backward and gestured toward the ten people standing to his right and spoke again.

"These men and women are the first to be trained as Guardians of Unity and more will be appointed as the need arises. I commission them before you today!"

A slow-growing applause began in the crowd. Some were confident, others less so, but everyone trusted Raan.

Again, Raan lifted his hand palm outward, and the people became still.

"Now we will have the opportunity show our unity to ourselves and to each other," said Raan, carefully and clearly.

"Before us is the basin of the Waters of One." He looked to his left at the stone pillar and basin. "Any man, woman, or child who puts their hand in this water becomes bonded with everyone else who places their hand in the water. It is a sacred symbol to remind us that each person has value regardless of how different they are from us." Raan walked to the basin and put his right hand in the water and drew it out allowing the excess water to drip over his head.

"Will the Guardians of Unity come forward!" said Raan.

Seth and Emma, Casy, GB and Kia, with two Qerds named Kip and Jeri, as well as an artisan named Belihasian, a tradesperson named Neumend, and a farmer named Kuptu came forward and stood facing each other in a circle around the stone pedestal and basin. The people waited to see what would happen.

At Raan's signal the ten Guardians placed their right hands in the water and everyone heard a muffled thunderclap as if it came from under the earth. As they lifted their hands above their heads to allow the droplets to run through their hair, a little of Jeri's water dripped onto Kip, and Kip instinctively flipped some of his water at Jeri, but missed him, hitting Casy in the face. Casy thought it was funny, so she grabbed a handful of water and dumped it on Jeri, but as she did, some splashed onto GB's pants who in turn returned a splash Casy's way hitting Kia and Emma in the crossfire. Soon they all joined the fray and to the astonishment of the crowd, the guardians engaged in a holy water fight, splashing and laughing as each playfully honored the other in unabated joy.

Raan turned to the crowd and shrugged his shoulders in dismay, but while his back was turned, the reveling Guardians picked up the basin and dumped the entire container over Raan's head. The crowd roared. The basin was refilled and everyone lined up to place their right hand in the Waters of One and take their chance to splash the leaders and each other. And so a new tradition was born where the people of the region gathered once a year during midsummer, to place their hands in the Waters of One as a symbol of unity and soak the leaders and each other in the water of playful love.

[44]
A Dash to Treasure

TIME PASSED, AND ORDINARY LIFE resumed. The silk farmers continued to thrive, weavers and artisans flourished, and the town continued to prosper in harmony. The region of Clallot became even more well-known for its prized garments and carpets.

Raan continued to live in his loft bed at the little house by the House of Hearing. He began taking long walks alone, during which he would think and pray. His wisdom and compassion deepened as he began to embrace the weight of responsibility the prince had placed upon him.

After many busy days, Raan remembered the map.

"How exciting!" said Casy, speaking for GB and Seth too.

"The adventure isn't over yet," said GB, boiling with enthusiasm. One adventure left, thought Raan, remembering the words of the Voice. Seth just smiled. So the four friends journeyed through the mountains and stood again in the castle courtyard. They stared at the map, trying to discover a landmark that could become a starting point.

"Remember the Prince's dying motions?" GB said. "One hand reached into his coat, but the other pointed toward Raan. Maybe he was pointing above where Raan was standing, to something behind him."

"Where were you exactly?" asked Casy.

Raan moved to where he'd stood that day, and they all looked. Immediately above where Raan stood, they saw the prince's coat of arms hung on a great wooden shield.

"It's the coat of arms from Zambo's picture," said GB.

"Yes, and I've seen that coat of arms before," Seth said, "in the Great Hall!"

They all rushed into the Great Hall, and there, intricately carved in a large oak panel, was the coat of arms.

"Look at the symbols on the coat of arms—they're the same as the pictograms on Zambo's picture! See three stars, a hammer, a sword, a plow, and a beaming sun."

"But they're in slightly different positions," said GB.

"But what does it mean?" asked Casy. The woman reached up and touched one of the stars and was astonished when it moved! The other stars moved, too, and so did all the other symbols.

"It's a puzzle! Zambo's been at it again!" said Raan, peering more intently at the picture and shifting his focus to the panel.

"Look at the positions of the stars, they're all rotated," GB said, pointing to the stars on the map.

"Let me try something," Casy said, reaching up on tiptoe, rotating each star to match the stars on the picture. They all heard a solid click inside the panel and held their breath, but nothing happened.

All their eyes focused on the picture and the following pictogram, the hammer.

GB pulled a stool over to stand face-to-face with the panel. He tested the hammer in all directions, and sure enough, it moved.

"Rotate it to match the pictogram on the picture," said Raan.

So GB rotated the hammer into position, and they all heard a second click.

"Let's try them all," said Casy. One by one, they found pictograms and moved the matching carvings until they were all amazed when the wood panel made a large clunking sound and swung inward, framing a doorway—blacker than black.

"Get some lamps!" said Casy.

"And don't forget extra oil," said Seth.

GB and Raan quickly returned with lamps and a flask of oil. They moved into the darkness and discovered a few torches near the entrance. Only Raan remained behind in the light, held by an unaccountable reluctance to go into the passage. He reached for the stone, but of course it was gone. He was alone in the light with his friends disappearing into the gloom.

"Wait!" Raan called. "Let me see the map!"

With the others looking on, Raan held out the parchment and pointed to a figure on the map. "This is where we are. And if we follow the line this way . . ." He pointed down the shadowed corridor. "Don't you see? The map is directions for the maze. If we carefully follow it . . ."

". . . it will show us the way to the treasure!" said GB and Casy in chorus.

"Not so fast," said Seth, holding back his excitement. "We need a lifeline to help lead us back in case we lose our light."

"I have just the thing," said Casy, who liked to knit while she was on long wagon rides. She found her bag in the wagon and produced a huge ball of yarn. "I've another just like it," said Casy, "We can tie it here and unwind it as we walk, then follow it back if we have trouble."

The four companions plunged into the secret passage, this time with Raan in the lead, then GB, followed by Casy, and Seth bringing up the rear, doling out the yarn. The shadows fled before the lamplight as the explorers followed carefully under arches, around corners, through doors, and down flights of stairs, avoiding some passages and entering others, sometimes walking, sometimes crawling, until they came into a vast cavern containing an underground lake.

Raan recognized the place where he'd almost drowned and realized they'd come into the cavern from another passage. "I've been here before, but it wasn't so beautiful," said Raan, staring at the glistening crystal formations on the walls and ceiling.

"They look like miniature fairy villages made with gems of glittering red, green, and blue," said GB.

They splashed through a small stream; in the torchlight, it looked like a carpet of moving glass.

The lake reflected the glowing light, revealing the dark openings of caves and other tunnels. Across the lake, Raan spied the wooden contraption he'd discovered before.

"Can I have a little light to see the map," Seth asked.

"Look, this line must be the path on the water's edge," said GB.

Casy, Seth, and GB hurried along the path, leaving Raan frozen and haunted by the dark memory of his encounter with the Voice. He ventured a whisper: "Are you here, Voice?" He waited, but all he heard were his friends:

"Come on, slowpoke!" shouted Casy. "We're almost there!"

Jolted out of his thoughts, Raan caught up until they stood near the wooden machine, half in and half out of the water. It towered above them.

They noticed a large, complicated mechanism of wooden wheels and beams supported by an intricate framework of ropes and pulleys. A canister was suspended from a long plank that resembled a lever, and three ropes hung down from above, spaced a dozen feet apart. The friends looked at each other and then back at the map.

"According to the map, we should be here," said GB.

"But what are these words at the bottom of the page?" Casy questioned. "'Together is the Key.'"

"It must be another riddle," said Raan, but he thought the contraption seemed like the game of Mouse Trap back home.

Walking to the water's edge, Seth filled an empty bucket and poured water into the suspended canister, saying, "This is obvious." They all watched the newly filled canister move the lever and heard sounds deep in the mechanism. But soon, it was all silent, the bucket on the lever emptied itself, and the lever returned to its original position. They all looked at Seth, who studied the curious machinery.

"Maybe it's broken," said GB.

"I don't think so," said Raan, looking at the map again. "It's another puzzle."

"What happens if we pull this rope?" said GB, walking to a rope dangling from a pulley on one side of the machine.

"Be careful!" said Seth, but GB pulled the rope before anyone could stop him.

"Look out!" yelled Casy as a gigantic pendulum swung from the shadows almost sweeping them into the lake. The ground vibrated with a colossal clunk, and the lake rippled, but the pendulum returned to its original position and locked in place.

"We must do it together, thinking about the words, to get the mechanism to work," interrupted Casy.

"What about this other rope?" asked GB.

"Everyone stand back before GB tries it," warned Seth.

When GB pulled the rope, it didn't budge, so Raan and GB tried together. With both pulling, the rope gave way, and they saw a giant wheel rotate and heard a clack, but nothing else happened.

Frustrated, GB blurted out a desperate prayer: "O Voice, we need help here. Show us what we need to do!"

Seth said, "Maybe we can do it together simultaneously. I'll pour the water, and GB and Raan will pull the ropes."

With renewed hope, they each went to their bucket or rope.

"On the count of three," said Casy.

The lads pulled with all their might, and Seth poured; the pendulum swung, but Raan's rope wouldn't budge. GB plopped to the floor, discouraged.

"The rope is too stiff to pull on my own," said Raan in frustration.

Seth shrugged as the lever shifted back. "Still, there's the third rope."

"I've got it!" Casy said. "Each of you grab a rope with one hand, and I'll stand between you, and we'll all hold hands and pull together.

They all sprang into action. Casy moved between Raan and GB, reached out, and realized their gap was still too big.

"Reach out with your crutch," said Raan.

Casy held her crutch end to Raan and gripped GB's other hand. They counted down from three, then pulled with all their might. Seth poured again, and they heard promising mechanical sounds that quickly disappeared.

"We still need the third rope," said Casy.

"But the three of us can't reach it while pulling the others," said Raan.

"And I can't reach the third rope while pouring, but I think it all must happen at once," said Seth, still searching for the solution.

The four friends stood utterly flummoxed, and Raan said a silent prayer. Then, a gentle breeze blew through the cavern, causing the third rope to swing a little.

"I've got it," yelled Seth, who was doing a little happy dance. "It's simple! The breeze blew the third rope and started it swinging."

He ran over and filled the spare bucket with water, tied it to the end of the third rope, and swung it toward his spot by the lever.

"Places, everyone!" called the Listener, as silly as a kid with a bag of candy.

The swinging bucket came near Seth, but he missed it by an inch. The next time, he caught the bucket handle and untied the third rope.

"Now pour and pull!" yelled Raan. Seth filled the canister, a long wooden key piece slid into position while pulling the third rope, and other cogs and levers moved as GB, Raan, and Casy pulled the other ropes via their human chain.

Suddenly, like clockwork, the powerful pendulum swung, and they heard wheels spinning, levers turning, chains moving, and clunking vibrations from beneath their feet while they held their grips. They also heard swirling water.

Seth said, "Look at the lake!"

A massive whirlpool swirled in the lake's center.

"It's getting bigger and bigger!"

"And look, the water's going down!"

The friends watched as the lake drained away, and they gasped when they noticed the lake bottom filled with dozens of barrels and chests. They all stood drop-jawed in amazement, but Raan noticed a speck of white half buried in the mud near the far edge of the empty pool. Immediately, he waded into the muck and pulled out a slimy silk string fastened to an oddly shaped white stone. For Raan, that was all the treasure he needed.

[45] UNBELIEVABLE!

WITH STEADY GUIDANCE from Seth and others who were now free to shine with fresh wisdom and ideas, things steadily improved. The Guardians helped people settle their disagreements, and people agreed that they felt better than they had in years. Raan reluctantly led the people in the prince's stead. He never fully accepted the title of prince but agreed to govern until a more permanent arrangement could be found.

They upgraded the schools and made them more accommodating to different styles of learning and made hospitals accessible to all. They expanded libraries and founded institutions to help create opportunities for everyone; and there were improvements to the area's museums and parks that exceeded everyone's expectations. The area prospered, driven by new ideas and the notion that everyone had something valuable to contribute.

The Bibgits kept their traditions and still lived in their colony, and the Qerds, artisans, farmers, and townspeople kept their ways, but the hostility between the races all but vanished, leaving only a few genial issues of personal preference and taste. There was free coming and going between town and colony, and the fruit of joy was everywhere.

Then, one day while the friends were walking together near the hay fields, Raan saw, a half mile down the road, a sight he'd long expected: the two men from the music shop approaching in their wagon. Raan knew it was time for him to leave, so he gulped, took a breath, and turned to face his dearest friends. "I have something to tell you that's really important but sad."

"I have something to say first," said Casy. "It's difficult, and it may be hard to understand, but please, don't think I'm crazy."

There was an awkward silence as the three men looked thoughtfully at the courageous woman who had warmed their hearts and propelled them to good deeds on all their adventures.

"I'm not from around here and have to leave. Raan and GB, you have become my best friends, and I will miss you."

The guys looked at her quizzically, and after a shy glance at them all, she spoke again: "I'm from another world and was sent here on a mission. I know what you're thinking but hear me out. It's not something I'm making up. It'd almost be easier if it were."

"Casy, that's crazy," Raan said, "but not in the way you think. I believe you. What mission?"

"To bring hope to the people."

Both lads looked shocked and stood there silently for what seemed an eternity.

"From where?" asked GB.

"From another life, another world. Different houses, streets, towns, and people, but I'm the same. That's what I can't figure out. Everyone seems to know me, but everything's strange. I've been learning as I go. Back home in my world, I was in a hospital after a horrible accident and lost everything; honestly, I didn't know what I was going to do with my life."

GB and Raan looked at her in wide-eyed wonder. In their eyes, she was a pillar of strength. Now, they were astonished to hear about what she'd been through.

GB said, "Casy, I believe you, and you won't believe it, but I'm from another world, too! I was sent to show perseverance. I'm a farm worker on my home world, helping to support my family. I had so much passion for people and the Good News of love but had no opportunity to go to college. This has been the grandest adventure! I've learned so much from you, Seth, and the challenges, but I think I need to go back."

Now Casy and GB look thoughtfully at Raan.

"We're sorry, but we need to go. The men in the wagon have come for us. We're sorry, but we both feel torn in two. Part of me wants to stay and help with the rebuilding of Clallot, but another part yearns to return and make the most out of my life where I left off," Casy said, holding back tears.

Then, with unusual enthusiasm, Raan said, "This is unbelievable! I'm from another world, too! I was sent to show each person has value."

The wagon pulled up to find the three friends gaping. Seth stood looking on with his hands in his pockets and a twinkle in his eye. He nodded to the two men as they drove away, with the three flabbergasted friends discussing their adventures. One by one, lulled by the sounds of the rhythm of the wheels and road, they dropped off to sleep as the wagon passed into a tunnel, and they were never seen in that world again.

[46]
23RD AND GRAMERCY PARK

RAAN WAS JOLTED AWAKE and found himself on a subway, smashed against a heavy woman with three noisy children in a crowd of overcoated people carrying messenger bags and backpacks. The screech of the subway brakes reverberated in the tiled tunnel. The station sign read 23rd Street - Gramercy Park. It was his stop!

He climbed the stairs to his flat two at a time and found the hidden key. It looked as if his cats hadn't missed him a bit. After plugging in his dead phone, declumping the litter box, and turning up the air purifier, he checked his news streams and realized it was the 18th of March, the day after he'd disappeared on his adventure. He learned that war still raged overseas and battles for public opinion raged at home, while the dirty, noisy, crowded, practically dysfunctional behemoth of lovable New York City remained unchanged.

But Raan was different. The stones and sidewalks, cars and cabs, trees and lampposts remained the same, yet the way he viewed people had changed. Raan no longer saw them as problems to avoid but as doorways into unique stories filled with meaning and a sense of purpose.

The next day, Raan woke up to the sound of church bells and smiled. Usually he'd be annoyed, but this morning he felt a calm curiosity as they rang, which made him want to learn about their meaning. But not today, he had a more urgent task—walk back to the Village Music Emporium, where his unusual adventure began.

Brimming with excitement, he shot down 3rd Ave., cutting across 18th Street to Park, past the bookstore and the many-colored awnings of vegetable sellers in Union Square Greenmarket. He avoided the dog run and zigzagged over to 12th, avoiding getting clobbered by a chocolate-covered long john dropped by a worker on a scaffold above the sidewalk. He gave some change to a street person as he turned south on 5th toward Washington Square Park and NYU, approaching the corner of Sullivan and Bleecker, the location of the storefront that had started his unusual journey.

But there he stood, dumbfounded. The music emporium was gone, and the storefront where it had been was now the Sullivan Street Tea & Spice Company. Aghast, Raan's heart dropped. The corner deli and gluten-free Italian restaurant were there, but the music shop had vanished.

"More magic," said Raan aloud. Out of habit, he reached and touched the center of his chest, feeling the familiar lump of the white stone. He drew it out and examined its strange markings. At least he knew the adventure wasn't a dream. He was glad it happened but sad it was over, and most of all, he missed his friends. He wondered where GB was and how Seth was doing, but most of all, he thought about Casy.

He moved in front of the tea shop window to look at the multicolored jars and boxes. New York was behind him, and he could see the reflection of parked cars and his melancholy face in the picture window. Looking deeper beyond the surface, he saw rows of neatly labeled jars of tea and spices that reminded him of the kitchen in Seth's cottage. If he could only try them all, thought Raan. Then he noticed the movement of a salesperson behind the counter. She was facing away from him, wearing a gray baseball cap and a black leather jacket over a blue jean dress. Standing on one foot, she reached for a high shelf, busy filling a package with tea from a jar. Then he saw something else: hanging by a hook near a rack of Himalayan pink salt cookware was an old wooden crutch.

~The End~

About the Author

Will Brooke, a native New Yorker, has devoted his career to the art of fixing things. His dedication has taken him across the globe, armed with a toolbox and sketchbook. His passion for drawing, inventing, and storytelling has been a constant from a young age, leading him to create imaginative worlds and build treehouses.

Brooke's writing is a product of the tranquil moments just after dawn, when the only sounds are birdsongs and a boiling kettle. His inspiration draws from classic adventure literature and modern masters like Orson Scott Card, Leif Enger, Tolkien, Lewis, and anything, natural or otherwise, that displays the fingerprints of God.

Brooke's life is a tapestry of diverse interests and experiences. He holds a Master of Arts from Wheaton College and currently resides near the Great Lakes in the United States. His love for good food, great books, family, friends, the vibrant city, and long walks is evident in his daily life. He is always on the lookout for hidden mysteries, be it in a book or on an adventure.

The Talking Stone is his debut novel.

Acknowledgements

Art thrives within a community. While an author's journey typically begins in solitude and contemplation, it truly comes to life through the support of friends and colleagues. I want to express my gratitude to the following individuals who have generously contributed to bringing this story to fruition. Their encouragement has made it possible for *The Talking Stone* to be published.

I want to thank the book's advance reading team for their time, suggestions, valuable comments, and reviews: George Ridgeway, Carol Tetzlaff, Tom Flaim, Cheri Pierson, Matt Woodley, David Cho, Bill MacKillop, Glauber Ribeiro, John Traynor, Joe Biondo, Ginny Emery, Carol Muzzy, Ron Shaffer, Will Triggs, Helen Wessel, and Anoill Youkhaneh.

I am also grateful to *The Talking Stone's* impeccable editorial team: Caleb Sjogren, Sheila Urban, and Virginia Emery of Given Word Books.

Finally, I appreciate the special encouragement and prayer support from Brooke Sanchez, Mary

Flores, the Wheaton, Indiana, and California Urbans, Jim and Margaret Bell, Ken and Carrol Muzzy, the Resurrection prayer team, and my very patient wife.

Windwalker Books Titles

Backward down the Mountain

Small Talks with God

40 Days with Jesus

Brill: The Tale of a Reluctant Donkey

Available at online retailers.

ENDORSEMENTS

Full of surprises, humor, and action!

"*The Talking Stone* is truly exceptional and is a great blend of magical realism and fantasy. I was completely drawn into the honest, pure-hearted, heroic story and devoured it in a weekend. The characters, too, are special—full of surprises, humor, and action. It will definitely be on my giving list!"

—Tom Flaim, best-selling author of the children's book series The Adventures of Uno, the Water Drop and Thirsty for Christ. *He is also the founder of Water@Work, which provides clean water relief on five continents.*

Sparkles with warmth and wit!

"*The Talking Stone* is a captivating adventure that blends imaginative storytelling with rich characters and timeless truths. I was drawn in from the very first chapter and quickly found myself cheering for Raan, Casy, GB, and Seth as they navigated danger, mystery, and moments of humor and heart. The world-building is vivid, and the dialogue sparkles with warmth and wit. I know my own grandchildren would be swept up in this tale and ask for 'just one more chapter.' This is the kind of story that stays with you long after the final page—an engaging read for kids, parents, and grandparents alike."

—Carol *Tetzlaff, award-winning author of* Ezra *and associate publisher, Redemption Press*

Thoughtfully edifying!

"I read it aloud to my eleven-year-old grandson, who begged for 'just one more chapter—pleeze!' at the end of each session. The short, punchy chapters held his interest. My young listener had numerous 'aha' moments when he wondered aloud about parallels with other stories. It's a joy to watch and hear a child interact with a story that stimulates on multiple levels. That's what *The Talking Stone* by Will Brooke does best—it's an exciting fantasy that challenges young readers to rise to new positive levels. My grandson's comment after finishing was, 'I want to read that by myself. There was a lot in there!' I heartily agree!"

—George Ridgeway (and grandson), spiritual director, submariner, and captain, Chaplain Corps, USN, retired

Highly recommended—I read it twice!

"Will Brooke's *The Talking Stone* is highly recommended for young readers (ages 11-17) who love adventure and learning about the meaning of life. The magically real fantasy is filled with plenty of twists and turns as Raan is sent on a mission to another world guided by a magical stone.

His mission becomes complicated by enemies who want to stop him and blame him for their evil deeds.

However with each encounter, Raan grows in courage, faith, and determination where he discovers life's meaning and the voice who truly guides him."

—Cheri Pierson, author, associate professor emerita, Wheaton College Graduate School

What a fun, rip-roaring tale!

"If you want a story with adventure, plucky characters, plot twists, suspense, sorrows, and setbacks interwoven with dashes of humor—this is it. Our hero, the young man Raan, enters another world where he meets an engaging band of friends and fellow heroes. Then this unlikely band faces danger, injustice, and corruption. They overcome it all with the power of goodness and faith, but it isn't an easy journey. And that's where the story gets really interesting. So take, read, and enjoy!"

—Matt Woodley, podcaster, journalist, author, pastor, and former editor of preachingtoday.com